THE GIRLS OF SLENDER MEANS

MURIEL SPARK DBE, CLit, FRSE, FRSL was born in Edinburgh in 1918. A poet, essayist, biographer and novelist, she won much international praise, receiving the James Tait Black Memorial Prize in 1965 for *The Mandelbaum Gate*, the US Ingersoll Foundation TS Eliot Award in 1992 and the David Cohen Prize in 1997. She was twice shortlisted for the Booker Prize (for *The Public Image* in 1969 and *Loitering with Intent* in 1981) and, in 2010, was shortlisted for the 'Lost Man Booker Prize' of 1970. In 1993 Muriel Spark was made a Dame for services to literature. In 1998 she was awarded the Golden PEN Award for a 'Lifetime's Distinguished Service to Literature'. She died in Tuscany in 2006.

ROSEMARY GORING, from Dunbar in East Lothian, took a degree in economic and social history at St Andrews University. She worked in publishing with W&R Chambers and Larousse before becoming a journalist. She was editor of *Life and Work*, the magazine of the Church of Scotland. She regularly adapts books for BBC Radio 4. A columnist for the *Herald*, she is also Literary Editor of the *Herald* and *Sunday Herald*, and on the board of the *Scottish Review of Books*, to which she is a regular contributor. Her books include *Scotland The Autobiography: 2,000 Years of Scottish History by Those Who Saw It Happen*, and the novels *After Flodden* and *Dacre's War*, set in riotous early sixteenth-century Scotland.

Novels by Muriel Spark in Polygon

THE GIRLS OF SLENDER MEANS

Muriel Spark

Introduced by Rosemary Goring

FT

This edition published in Great Britain in 2018
by Polygon, an imprint of Birlinn Ltd.

Birlinn Ltd
West Newington House
10 Newington Road
Edinburgh
EH9 1QS

www.polygonbooks.co.uk

3

ISBN 978 1 84697 431 1

The publisher gratefully acknowledges investment from
Creative Scotland towards the publication of this book.

Supported by the Muriel Spark Society

British Library Cataloguing-in-Publication Data
A catalogue record for this book is available
on request from the British Library.

Typeset by Biblichor Ltd, Edinburgh
Printed and bound in Malta by Gutenberg Press

Foreword

Muriel Spark was born in Edinburgh on the first of February, 1918. She was the second child of Cissy and Bernard Camberg, an engineer from a family of Jewish and Lithuanian extraction. Her early life is recalled in loving and meticulous detail in her autobiography, *Curriculum Vitae*, published in 1992. Hers was a working-class upbringing, but while money was tight she was in no way deprived. Her mother was gregarious and extrovert, always singing songs and telling stories, and wearing the kind of clothes that made her unmissable among other, more dully dressed women in the Bruntsfield neighbourhood.

When she was five years old Spark began her education at James Gillespie's High School for Girls where she remained until she was sixteen. It was a period she remembered with great fondness. She was anointed the school's 'Poet and Dreamer' and many of her early verses appeared in its magazine. In 1929, she first encountered an inspirational teacher, a spinster called Christina Kay, who was to have a formative effect on her life. It was Miss Kay, for example, who took her and her friends – 'the crème de la crème' – on long walks through the city's Old Town, to exhibitions, concerts and poetry readings, and who insisted that she must become a writer. 'I felt I had hardly much choice in the matter,' Spark wrote later. In her sixth and most famous novel, *The Prime of Miss Jean Brodie*, the main character was modelled closely, if not actually, on Miss Kay. Like the unorthodox Miss Brodie, Miss Kay was an Italophile and a naive admirer of Mussolini, of whom she pinned a picture on a wall together with paintings by Renaissance masters.

On leaving school Spark enrolled in a course for précis-writing at Heriot-Watt College. She then found a job as secretary to the owner of a department store in Princes Street, the Scottish capital's main thoroughfare. At a dance she met Sydney Oswald Spark, a lapsed Jew, whose initials she felt in hindsight should have warned her to steer clear of him. Like her father's parents, 'SOS' had been born in Lithuania. She was nineteen, he was thirty-two. He planned to teach in Africa, and Muriel, eager to leave Edinburgh and launch herself at life, agreed to become engaged. In August 1937, she followed him to Southern Rhodesia (now Zimbabwe) and the following month they were married. Their son, Robin, was born in 1938. Soon thereafter the couple separated.

The outbreak of war the following year meant Spark could not return home as she had hoped and she had no option but to stay in Africa. In 1944, however, she obtained a divorce and returned to Britain on a troop ship. Having settled her son with her parents, she headed for London where the devastation of the Blitz was everywhere evident. She boarded at the Helena Club, the original of the May of Teck Club in *The Girls of Slender Means*, and found work in the Political Intelligence department of the Foreign Office, whose *raison d'être* was to disseminate anti-Nazi propaganda among the German population.

In the years immediately after the war she attempted to make a living as a writer. In 1947, she was appointed General Secretary of the Poetry Society and editor of its magazine, *Poetry Review*, but she fell foul of traditionalists, including Marie Stopes, a pioneer of birth control. It was a pity, Spark remarked, 'that her mother rather than she had not thought of birth control'. Her first book, *A Tribute to Wordsworth*, was co-written with her then lover, Derek Stanford, and published in 1950. A year later she won a short story competition in the *Observer* newspaper with 'The Seraph and the Zambesi'. In 1952, she published her debut collection of poetry, *The Fanfarlo and Other Verse*.

Her conversion to Catholicism in 1954 coincided with her beginning work on her first novel, *The Comforters*, which finally appeared in 1957. Praised by Graham Greene and Evelyn Waugh among others, it allowed Spark to give up part-time secretarial work and devote herself to writing. Four more novels – *Robinson*, *Memento Mori*, *The Ballad of Peckham Rye* and *The Bachelors*, and a collection of stories, *The Go-Away Bird* – followed in quick succession and enhanced her reputation for originality and wit.

It was with the publication in 1961 of *The Prime of Miss Jean Brodie*, however, that Spark became an international bestseller. It was turned into a play and a film for which Maggie Smith, who played the eponymous teacher, won the Oscar for Best Actress. Indeed, remarked Spark, so closely did Smith become associated with the part that many readers seemed to assume that she was her creator. The novel, which Spark liked to refer to as her 'milch cow', was a critical as well as a commercial success and continued to sell well throughout its author's long career. In America, it was first published in the *New Yorker*. Its editor, William Shawn, gave Spark an office in which to work. There, she wrote her next two novels, *The Girls of Slender Means* and *The Mandelbaum Gate*, which was awarded the James Tait Black Memorial Prize.

In 1967, having grown tired of the clamour and claustrophobia of life in New York, she moved to Italy and Rome.

That same year she was made an OBE. It also saw the publication of her first collected volumes of stories and poems. Novels continued to appear at regular intervals. *The Public Image* appeared in 1968 and was shortlisted for the Booker Prize. *The Driver's Seat*, which Spark believed to be her best, was published in 1970. In 1974 came *The Abbess of Crewe*, an inspired satire of the Watergate scandal, which she set in a convent.

In the mid 1970s Spark left Rome for Tuscany, settling in a rambling and venerable house deep in the countryside, owned by her friend, Penelope Jardine, an artist. Surrounded by fields of vines and olives, she was able to work without fear of interruption. *The Takeover*, *Territorial Rights* and *Loitering with Intent* – also shortlisted for the Booker – were among the first novels she wrote in the place that would be her final home. Among the many awards she received were the Ingersoll Foundation TS Eliot Award, the Scottish Arts Council Award for *Reality and Dreams*, the Boccaccio Prize for European Literature, the David Cohen British Literature Prize for a lifetime's achievement, and the Golden PEN Award from PEN International. In 1993, she was made a Dame.

Though in her later years she was often beset by illness, she never stopped writing. It was her calling and she pursued it with unfailing dedication. She always had a poem 'on the go' and she never wanted for ideas for novels and stories and plays. Among her later novels were *A Far Cry from Kensington*, *Symposium*, *Reality and Dreams* and *Aiding and Abetting*. Her valedictory novel was *The Finishing School*, the majority of whose characters are would-be writers, which was published in 2004. Spark died two years later at the age of eighty-eight and is buried in the walled cemetery of the village of Oliveto in the Val di Chiana. On her headstone, she is described in Italian with one simple word: *poeta*.

Introduction

Rosemary Goring

'Bombed-out London was the first real London I was to know,' wrote Muriel Spark in her autobiography, *Curriculum Vitae*. She had recently returned to Britain from what was then Rhodesia, on a perilous journey by troop ship. With its cargo of soldiers and thirty intrepid civilian women, the ship zigzagged from Cape Town to Liverpool via the Azores in order to avoid German U-boats. 'On this, as on other occasions during the war,' she later wrote, 'being "in it together" took the edge off fear.'

This collegiate spirit infuses *The Girls of Slender Means*, which draws heavily on her experience of a city ravaged by bombs, the populace growing thin and tetchy as rations tightened, yet refusing to buckle under the strain. At the start of the novel, the omniscient narrator reflects on the sight of buildings reduced to rubble, of craters and apartment blocks ripped open to public view like dolls' houses: 'There was absolutely no point in feeling depressed about the scene, it would have been like feeling depressed about the Grand Canyon.'

It was several weeks before Spark found a job in the Foreign Office in its hush-hush department of Black Propaganda, in which she helped concoct bogus news stories to lower the German population's morale and undermine trust in their leaders. During this time she boarded in the Helena Club, a genteel hostel for women. Even after she got the Foreign Office job and took lodgings in Woburn, Spark returned there during her leave, hungry for the glamour of upmarket hotels, good restaurants and the cheering dance floors of blacked-out London. In this the occupants of her fictional club have much in common with her.

The Helena Club, at 82 Lancaster Gate, was a relic of a more punctilious, proper age. Originally established by one of Queen Victoria's daughters for 'Ladies from Good Families of Modest Means who are Obliged to Pursue an Occupation in London', it is transformed in *The Girls of Slender Means* into the May of Teck Club, a similar institution, in the same location, whose upper floors overlook Kensington Gardens. This district was to feature in other fictional works of Spark, and in this tale there are precursors and intimations of characters and situations found in her much later novel, *A Far Cry from Kensington*, set a decade after the war, when things were dramatically different. In certain respects, though, it was an equally or even more dreary time.

Despite the terrors, tedium and deprivations of 1945, the year in which the main story of *The Girls of Slender Means* takes place, the youthful tenants of the May of Teck Club set the story alight with their high spirits, aspirations, eccentricities and foolishness. There is fat Jane Wright, who works in publishing, but later becomes a newspaper columnist. She needs all the food she can lay her hands on, because of the demands of her 'brain work'; there is unutterably beautiful Selina Redwood, who daily recites an incantation to make her even more elegant as if it were the Angelus ('Poise is perfect balance, an equanimity of body and mind . . .'); there is 'mad' Pauline Fox who dines regularly with an imaginary companion, the well-known actor Jack Buchanan; and lively, worldly Anne, whose coveted Schiaparelli taffeta evening dress is the envy of the whole house, and shared between the young women in return for ration cards or other desirable items, such as a sliver of soap. Of course, only the slender can wear it. And, more importantly still, only the slimmest of this elite are svelte enough to slip through the lavatory window onto the flat roof where they can sunbathe or – like Selina – spend the night with a lover. That narrow window, like that dress, is to carry a profound spiritual significance, Spark brilliantly and mercilessly conflating down-to-earth and frivolous reality with deep and disturbing metaphysics. This ability to move seamlessly between both spheres is a speciality of her rare, exceptional talent, and gives this novel its unsettling, shocking power.

Among the heedless, self-obsessed girls in the May of Teck are a handful who are more mature, either in years or outlook. Most intriguing is the preternaturally devout and attractive vicar's daughter Joanna Childe, thwarted in love and determined to nurse her misery to keep it warm. An elocution teacher, her voice is the descant to this novel, heard mostly off-stage as she recites or puts her pupils through their exercises. The chapters are punctuated by snatches of Wordsworth, Blake, Tennyson and Coleridge, among many others. Particularly poignant and prophetic is her much-praised rendition of Gerard Manley Hopkins's 'The Wreck of the Deutschland', which he dedicated to the five nuns who drowned aboard that ship. The perpetual interjections of poetry – 'And all my days are trances', 'Now sleeps the crimson petal, now the white', 'Like one, that on a lonesome road . . .' – are beads on the rosary of this contemplative and, to use the narrator's own word, savage story. As Spark writes of the club's inmates, 'Few people alive at the time were more delightful, more ingenious, more movingly lovely, and, as it might happen, more savage, than the girls of slender means.'

One or two long-term residents are in their fifties, despite the May of Teck's age-limit of thirty. It is one of these elders, Greggie, who points out the declivity in the garden where a bomb fell in '42. 'It's my suspicion there was a second bomb that didn't go off. I'm almost sure I saw it drop as I picked myself up off the floor,' she likes to tell newcomers. Thus the sinister seed of doubt and danger is sown.

As with all her fiction, Spark dresses her stage like a theatre director, and moves her characters accordingly. There is a palpable sense as *The Girls of Slender Means* opens of the curtain rising, catching people in mid-conversation, in half-spoken sentences, and banal acts that, ordinary though they seem, prove to be telling. A slender novel it might be, but every word has heft.

All enclosed communities attract incomers, foxes in the coop who set feathers flying. This role falls to the poet Nicholas Farringdon, who is friends with all the young women, but besotted by Selina, whose soul he hopes to awaken. The novel opens with the news, nearly twenty years after the war, that he has been martyred in Haiti, where he was a missionary. Told in flashback from the present-day –1963 – as the former housemates learn of his murder, a knowing tone is allowed to infuse what might otherwise appear to be disjointed vignettes. Gradually, as the drama escalates, to the soundtrack of Joanna's operatic recitations, it becomes clear that everything we are shown is a station of the cross on Nicholas Farringdon's path to Catholic conversion, and the spur for his vocation and eventual death. Slowly, too, one realises that only Nicholas had the full measure of what was going on in the May of Teck, and the wider world beyond.

This was Spark's seventh novel, published in November 1963, in the wake of *The Prime of Miss Jean Brodie*, which had come out two years before. It was, thus, the first novel she wrote when she was famous, conditions she had never before worked under. Late in July 1962, she took herself off for a couple of weeks to Aylesford Priory, a Carmelite retreat in Kent for Catholic artists who needed breathing space, and where she could find peace to write. But it was not her public from whom she was escaping. This was a sad and troubled time, following the death of her father earlier in the year, and acrimony with her son Robin. There is a hint that in writing *The Girls of Slender Means*, Spark was immersing herself in a world in which she had been a great deal more comfortable than the present, a period when dangers were prosaic and fathomable compared to the flak she was now taking on other fronts. Perhaps exhausted by the demands made upon her by family and friends, or maybe simply in need of a change of scene, Spark moved to New York part-way through writing. It was in her corner office at the *New Yorker* – a room she customised to her own stylish, colourful taste – that she wrote most of the novel, in November of that year. When she looked up from her notebook, she could see from her eighteenth-floor windows the flashing neon sign, *Time/Life*, on the Rockefeller Center. This view was a far cry from the emblematic needle-thin window of the May of Teck Club through which her girls had to clamber, but the message was oddly apposite.

The storm clouds of the Cuban Missile crisis and the Cold War were gathering as she wrote, but it is on the main dates of the Second World War that the themes of *The Girls of Slender Means* hang. Opening a few days after the VE Day celebrations on 8 May 1945, rising to a crescendo after the General Election of July, in which Churchill was ousted, and fading out with London's seething VJ Day party on the night of 15 August 1945, it is one of very few immediate post-war novels by a novelist who lived through it. In this respect it keeps company with Evelyn Waugh's *Sword of Honour* trilogy, Anthony Powell's *Dance to the Music of Time* series, and Henry Green's novels *Loving* and *Back*. Unlike these, Spark's interest in the period is not as social, sexual or political history, or anti-establishment satire, although these elements are all present. Her true focus, made explicitly plain here, was the nature of salvation. This, one of her abiding interests, is set within a wider questioning of the existential and spiritual import of this particular war, and its place in the grander scheme of world history and current affairs – events which, even after both armistices, continued to unfold at alarming speed.

Within this deceptively lightly-told meringue of a tale, the layers of enfolded meaning are abundant and complex. A single reading is not sufficient to glean everything that is being suggested or revealed. According to Martin Stannard, Spark's biographer, most reviewers struggled with 'the metaphysical dimension'. Those with discernment, however, such as John Updike, got it at once. He likened its clarity and mysteriousness to Kafka. Common readers, meanwhile, perhaps more perceptive than the critical community, and certainly no less so, leapt upon it, and within a few months it was a best-seller in Britain and America. That three days after publication, on 22 November, John F. Kennedy was assassinated merely heightened the relevance – if that actually mattered – of the dispassionate horror, acceptance of violence and eternal perspective it offers.

Spark's poetic title is open, typically, to several interpretations. Spiritual poverty and attempts to overcome this are the bedrock, but poverty in the ordinary sense is almost as important. Opening with the declaration that 'Long ago in 1945 all the nice people in England were poor', each chapter gives examples of the privations these young women must endure and the self-control they must exercise in order to survive, or give a passable impersonation of surviving. Ration cards are counted as carefully as calories by these sparrow-like creatures, who would stop at nothing to acquire additional supplies of tea or eggs or sweets. The counterpoint to such punishing austerity, however, was an appetite for life hard to match in peace-time. 'Love and money were the vital themes in all the bedrooms and dormitories,' writes Spark, but the greatest of these, or so it seems to this reader, was money. Few things are more wearying, mentally and for the spirit, than genuine hardship. On this subject, Spark knew of what she wrote. Nevertheless, necessity is a creative force. By rubbing two pennies together she struck sparks that transformed penury into a tinder-box of possibilities – a word all too appropriate for the residents, blessed and doomed, of the May of Teck.

So might there have been an upside to these days of slender means? Nicholas Farringdon possibly speaks for the author when he reflects, 'Poverty differs vastly from want'. A letter Spark received after publication of *The Girls of Slender Means* suggests there was much amusement to be found amid the scrimping and saving. Una Pinder, an old friend from Rhodesian days, when Muriel had left her husband, writes, 'Are brassieres still the most important item in your wardrobe!? Do you still scream for a taxi when you are stony-broke? Do you still, *still* burn your dress on the radiator once a year and use the claim money for your month's food!?'.

It does not need an Enigma code-breaker to read between the lines of this affectionate letter and catch an echo of laughter, fun and mischievous gaiety. And for all the soul-searching found in this novel, and its terrible glimpses of evil, it is a book that rings with merriment. There is no pleasure in poverty, but those whose means are slender when they are young are often richer than most in hope and in prospects – in this world, if not the next.

I

Long ago in 1945 all the nice people in England were poor, allowing for exceptions. The streets of the cities were lined with buildings in bad repair or in no repair at all, bomb-sites piled with stony rubble, houses like giant teeth in which decay had been drilled out, leaving only the cavity. Some bomb-ripped buildings looked like the ruins of ancient castles until, at a closer view, the wallpapers of various quite normal rooms would be visible, room above room, exposed, as on a stage, with one wall missing; sometimes a lavatory chain would dangle over nothing from a fourth- or fifth-floor ceiling; most of all the staircases survived, like a new art-form, leading up and up to an unspecified destination that made unusual demands on the mind's eye. All the nice people were poor; at least, that was a general axiom, the best of the rich being poor in spirit.

There was absolutely no point in feeling depressed about the scene, it would have been like feeling depressed about the Grand Canyon or some event of the earth outside every-body's scope. People continued to exchange assurances of depressed feelings about the weather or the news, or the Albert Memorial which had not been hit, not even shaken, by any bomb from first to last.

The May of Teck Club stood obliquely opposite the site of the Memorial, in one of a row of tall houses which had endured, but barely; some bombs had dropped near by, and in a few back gardens, leaving the buildings cracked on the outside and shakily hinged within, but habitable for the time being. The shattered windows had been replaced with new glass rattling in loose frames. More recently, the bituminous black-out paint had been removed from landing and bathroom windows. Windows were important in that year of final reckoning; they told at a glance whether a house was inhabited or not; and in the course of the past years they had accumulated much meaning, having been the main danger-zone between domestic life and the war going on outside: everyone had said, when the sirens sounded, 'Mind the windows. Keep away from the windows. Watch out for the glass.'

The May of Teck Club had been three times window-shattered since 1940, but never directly hit. There the windows of the upper bedrooms overlooked the dip and rise of treetops in Kensington Gardens across the street, with the Albert Memorial to be seen by means of a slight craning and twist of the neck. These upper bedrooms looked down on the opposite pavement on the park side of the street, and on the tiny people who moved along in neat-looking singles and couples, pushing little prams loaded with pin-head babies and provisions, or carrying little dots of shopping bags. Everyone carried a shopping bag in case they should be lucky enough to pass a shop that had a sudden stock of something off the rations.

From the lower-floor dormitories the people in the street looked larger, and the paths of the park were visible. All the nice people were poor, and few were nicer, as nice people come, than these girls at Kensington who glanced out of the windows in the early mornings to see what the day looked like, or gazed out on the green summer evenings, as if reflecting on the months ahead, on love and the relations of love. Their eyes gave out an eager-spirited light that resembled near-genius, but was youth merely. The first of the Rules of Constitution, drawn up at some remote and innocent Edwardian date, still applied more or less to them:

> The May of Teck Club exists for the Pecuniary Convenience and Social Protection of Ladies of Slender Means below the age of Thirty Years, who are obliged to reside apart from their Families in order to follow an Occupation in London.

As they realised themselves in varying degrees, few people alive at the time were more delightful, more ingenious, more movingly lovely, and, as it might happen, more savage, than the girls of slender means.

'I've got something to tell you,' said Jane Wright, the woman columnist.

At the other end of the telephone, the voice of Dorothy Markham, owner of the flourishing model agency, said, 'Darling, where have you been?' She spoke, by habit since her débutante days, with the utmost enthusiasm of tone.

'I've got something to tell you. Do you remember Nicholas Farringdon? Remember he used to come to the old May of Teck just after the war, he was an anarchist and poet sort of thing. A tall man with –'

'The one that got on to the roof to sleep out with Selina?'

'Yes, Nicholas Farringdon.'

'Oh rather. Has he turned up?'

'No, he's been martyred.'

'What-ed?'

'Martyred in Haiti. Killed. Remember he became a Brother –'

'But I've just been to Tahiti, it's marvellous, everyone's marvellous. Where did you hear it?'

'Haiti. There's a news paragraph just come over Reuters. I'm sure it's the same Nicholas Farringdon because it says a missionary, former poet. I nearly died. I knew him well, you know, in those days. I expect they'll hush it all up, about those days, if they want to make a martyr story.'

'How did it happen, is it gruesome?'

'Oh, I don't know, there's only a paragraph.'

'You'll have to find out more through your grapevine. I'm shattered. I've got heaps to tell you.'

The Committee of Management wishes to express surprise at the Members' protest regarding the wallpaper chosen for the drawing room. The Committee wishes to point out that Members' residential fees do not meet the running expenses of the Club. The Committee regrets that the spirit of the May of Teck foundation has apparently so far deteriorated that such a protest has been made. The Committee refers Members to the terms of the Club's Foundation.

Joanna Childe was a daughter of a country rector. She had a good intelligence and strong obscure emotions. She was training to be a teacher of elocution and, while attending a school of drama, already had pupils of her own. Joanna Childe had been drawn to this profession by her good voice and love of poetry which she loved rather as it might be assumed a cat loves birds; poetry, especially the declamatory sort, excited and possessed her; she would pounce on the stuff, play with it quivering in her mind, and when she had got it by heart, she spoke it forth with devouring relish. Mostly, she indulged the habit while giving elocution lessons at the club where she was highly thought of for it. The vibrations of Joanna's elocution voice from her room or from the recreation room where she frequently rehearsed, were felt to add tone and style to the establishment when boy-friends called. Her taste in poetry became the accepted taste of the club. She had a deep feeling for certain passages in the authorised version of the Bible, besides the Book of Common Prayer, Shakespeare and Gerard Manley Hopkins, and had newly discovered Dylan Thomas. She was not moved by the poetry of Eliot and Auden, except for the latter's lyric:

> Lay your sleeping head, my love,
> Human on my faithless arm;

Joanna Childe was large, with light shiny hair, blue eyes and deep-pink cheeks. When she read the notice signed by Lady Julia Markham, chairwoman of the committee, she stood with the other young women round the green baize board and was given to murmur: 'He rageth, and again he rageth, because he knows his time is short.'

It was not known to many that this was a reference to the Devil, but it caused amusement. She had not intended it so. It was not usual for Joanna to quote anything for its aptitude, and at conversational pitch.

Joanna, who was now of age, would henceforth vote conservative in the elections, which at that time in the May of Teck Club was associated with a desirable order of life that none of the members was old enough to remember from direct experience. In principle they all approved of what the committee's notice stood for. And so Joanna was alarmed by the amused reaction to her quotation, the hearty laugh of understanding that those days were over when the members of anything whatsoever might not raise their voices against the drawing-room wallpaper. Principles regardless, everyone knew that the notice was plain damned funny. Lady Julia must be feeling pretty desperate.

'He rageth and again he rageth, because he knows his time is short.'

Little dark Judy Redwood who was a shorthand typist in the Ministry of Labour said, 'I've got a feeling that as members we're legally entitled to a say in the administration. I must ask Geoffrey.' This was the man Judy was engaged to. He was still in the forces, but had qualified as a solicitor before being called up. His sister, Anne Baberton, who stood with the notice-board group, said, 'Geoffrey would be the last person I would consult.' Anne Baberton said this to indicate that she knew Geoffrey better than Judy knew him; she said it to indicate affectionate scorn; she said it because it was the obvious thing for a nicely brought-up sister to say, since she was proud of him; and besides all this, there was an element of irritation in her words, 'Geoffrey would be the last person I would consult', for she knew there was no point in members taking up this question of the drawing-room wallpaper.

Anne trod out her cigarette-end contemptuously on the floor of the large entrance hall with its pink and grey Victorian tiles. This was pointed to by a thin middle-aged woman, one of the few older, if not exactly the earliest members. She said, 'One is not permitted to put cigarette-ends on the floor.' The words did not appear to impress themselves on the ears of the group, more than the ticking of the grandfather clock behind them. But Anne said, 'Isn't one permitted to spit on the floor, even?' 'One certainly isn't,' said the spinster. 'Oh, I thought one was,' said Anne.

The May of Teck Club was founded by Queen Mary before her marriage to King George the Fifth, when she was Princess May of Teck. On an afternoon between the engagement and the marriage, the Princess had been induced to come to London and declare officially open the May of Teck Club which had been endowed by various gentle forces of wealth.

None of the original Ladies remained in the club. But three subsequent members had been permitted to stay on past the stipulated age-limit of thirty, and were now in their fifties, and had resided at the May of Teck Club since before the First World War at which time, they said, all members had been obliged to dress for dinner.

Nobody knew why these three women had not been asked to leave when they had reached the age of thirty. Even the warden and committee did not know why the three remained. It was now too late to turn them out with decency. It was too late even to mention to them the subject of their continuing residence. Successive committees before 1939 had decided that the three older residents might, in any case, be expected to have a good influence on the younger ones.

During the war the matter had been left in abeyance, since the club was half empty; in any case members' fees were needed, and bombs were then obliterating so much and so many in the near vicinity that it was an open question whether indeed the three spinsters would remain upright with the house to the end. By 1945 they had seen much coming of new girls and going of old, and were generally liked by the current batch, being subject to insults when they interfered in anything, and intimate confidences when they kept aloof. The confidences seldom represented the whole truth, particularly those revealed by the young women who occupied the top floor. The three spinsters were, through the ages, known and addressed as Collie (Miss Coleman), Greggie (Miss Macgregor) and Jarvie (Miss Jarman). It was Greggie who

7

had said to Anne by the notice-board: 'One isn't permitted to put cigarette-ends on the floor.'

'Isn't one permitted to spit on the floor, even?'

'No, one isn't.'

'Oh, I thought one was.'

Greggie affected an indulgent sigh and pushed her way through the crowd of younger members. She went to the open door, set in a wide porch, to look out at the summer evening like a shopkeeper waiting for custom. Greggie always behaved as if she owned the club.

The gong was about to sound quite soon. Anne kicked her cigarette-stub into a dark corner.

Greggie called over her shoulder, 'Anne, here comes your boy-friend.'

'On time, for once,' said Anne, with the same pretence of scorn that she had adopted when referring to her brother Geoffrey: 'Geoffrey would be the last person I would consult.' She moved, with her casual hips, towards the door.

A square-built high-coloured young man in the uniform of an English captain came smiling in. Anne stood regarding him as if he was the last person in the world she would consult.

'Good evening,' he said to Greggie as a well-brought-up man would naturally say to a woman of Greggie's years standing in the doorway. He made a vague nasal noise of recognition to Anne, which if properly pronounced would have been 'Hallo'. She said nothing at all by way of greeting. They were nearly engaged to be married.

'Like to come in and see the drawing-room wallpaper?' Anne said then.

'No, let's get cracking.'

Anne went to get her coat off the banister where she had slung it. He was saying to Greggie, 'Lovely evening, isn't it?'

8

Anne returned with her coat slung over her shoulder. 'Bye, Greggie,' she said. 'Goodbye,' said the soldier. Anne took his arm.

'Have a nice time,' said Greggie.

The dinner-gong sounded and there was a scuffle of feet departing from the notice-board and a scamper of feet from the floors above.

On a summer night during the previous week the whole club, forty-odd women, with any young men who might happen to have called that evening, had gone like swift migrants into the dark cool air of the park, crossing its wide acres as the crow flies in the direction of Buckingham Palace, there to express themselves along with the rest of London on the victory in the war with Germany. They clung to each other in twos and threes, fearful of being trampled. When separated, they clung to, and were clung to by, the nearest person. They became members of a wave of the sea, they surged and sang until, at every half-hour interval, a light flooded the tiny distant balcony of the Palace and four small straight digits appeared upon it: the King, the Queen, and the two Princesses. The royal family raised their right arms, their hands fluttered as in a slight breeze, they were three candles in uniform and one in the recognisable fur-trimmed folds of the civilian queen in war-time. The huge organic murmur of the crowd, different from anything like the voice of animate matter but rather more a cataract or a geological disturbance, spread through the parks and along the Mall. Only the St John's Ambulance men, watchful beside their vans, had any identity left. The royal family waved, turned to go, lingered and waved again, and finally disappeared. Many strange arms were twined round strange bodies. Many liaisons, some permanent, were formed in the night, and numerous infants of experimental variety, delightful in hue of skin and racial structure, were born to the world in the due cycle of nine months after. The bells pealed. Greggie observed that it was something between a wedding and a funeral on a world scale.

The next day everyone began to consider where they personally stood in the new order of things.

Many citizens felt the urge, which some began to indulge, to insult each other, in order to prove something or to test their ground.

The government reminded the public that it was still at war. Officially this was undeniable, but except to those whose relations lay in the Far-Eastern prisons of war, or were stuck in Burma, that war was generally felt to be a remote affair.

A few shorthand typists at the May of Teck Club started to apply for safer jobs – that is to say, in private concerns, not connected with the war like the temporary Ministries where many of them had been employed.

Their brothers and men friends in the forces, not yet demobilised, by a long way, were talking of vivid enterprises for the exploitation of peace, such as buying a lorry and building up from it a transport business.

'I've got something to tell you,' said Jane.

'Just a minute till I shut the door. The kids are making a row,' Anne said. And presently, when she returned to the telephone, she said, 'Yes, carry on.'

'Do you remember Nicholas Farringdon?'

'I seem to remember the name.'

'Remember I brought him to the May of Teck in nineteen forty-five, he used to come often for supper. He got mixed up with Selina.'

'Oh, Nicholas. The one who got up on the roof? What a long time ago that was. Have you seen him?'

'I've just seen a news item that's come over Reuters. He's been killed in a local rising in Haiti.'

'Really? How awful! What was he doing there?'

'Well, he became a missionary or something.'

'No!'

'Yes. It's terribly tragic. I knew him well.'

'Ghastly. It brings everything back. Have you told Selina?'

'Well, I haven't been able to get her. You know what Selina's like these days, she won't answer the phone personally, you have to go through thousands of secretaries or whatever they are.'

'You could get a good story for your paper out of it, Jane,' Anne said.

'I know that. I'm just waiting to get more details. Of course it's all those years ago since I knew him, but it would be an interesting story.'

Two men – poets by virtue of the fact that the composition of poetry was the only consistent thing they had so far done – beloved of two May of Teck girls and, at the moment, of nobody else, sat in their corduroy trousers in a café in Bayswater with their silent listening admirers and talked about the new future as they flicked the page-proofs of an absent friend's novel. A copy of *Peace News* lay on the table between them. One of the men said to the other:

And now what will become of us without Barbarians? Those
people were some sort of a solution.

And the other smiled, bored-like, but conscious that very few in all the great metropolis and its tributary provinces were as yet privy to the source of these lines. This other who smiled was Nicholas Farringdon, not yet known or as yet at all likely to be.

'Who wrote that?' said Jane Wright, a fat girl who worked for a publisher and who was considered to be brainy but somewhat below standard, socially, at the May of Teck.

Neither man replied.

'Who wrote that?' Jane said again.

The poet nearest her said, through his thick spectacles, 'An Alexandrian poet.'

'A new poet?'

'No, but fairly new to this country.'

'What's his name?'

He did not reply. The young men had started talking again. They talked about the decline and fall of the anarchist movement on the island of their birth in terms of the personalities concerned. They were bored with educating the girls for this evening.

2

Joanna Childe was giving elocution lessons to Miss Harper, the cook, in the recreation room. When she was not giving lessons she was usually practising for her next examination. The house frequently echoed with Joanna's rhetoric. She got six shillings an hour from her pupils, five shillings if they were May of Teck members. Nobody knew what her arrangements were with Miss Harper, for at that time all who kept keys of food-cupboards made special arrangements with all others. Joanna's method was to read each stanza herself first and make her pupil repeat it.

Everyone in the drawing-room could hear the loud lesson in progress beating out the stresses and throbs of *The Wreck of the Deutschland*.

> The frown of his face
> Before me, the hurtle of hell
> Behind, where, where was a, where was a place?

The club was proud of Joanna Childe, not only because she chucked up her head and recited poetry, but because she was so well built, fair and healthy looking, the poetic essence of tall, fair rectors' daughters who never used a scrap of make-up, who had served tirelessly day and night in parish welfare organisations since leaving school early in the war, who before that had been Head Girl and who never wept that anyone knew or could imagine, being stoical by nature.

What had happened to Joanna was that she had fallen in love with a curate on leaving school. It had come to nothing. Joanna had decided that this was to be the only love of her life.

She had been brought up to hear, and later to recite,

> . . . Love is not love
> Which alters when it alteration finds,
> Or bends with the remover to remove:

All her ideas of honour and love came from the poets. She was vaguely acquainted with distinctions and sub-distinctions of human and divine love, and their various attributes, but this was picked up from rectory conversations when theologically-minded clerics came to stay; it was in a different category of instruction from ordinary household beliefs such as the axiom, 'People are holier who live in the country', and the notion that a nice girl should only fall in love once in her life.

It seemed to Joanna that her longing for the curate must have been unworthy of the name of love, had she allowed a similar longing, which she began to feel, for the company of a succeeding curate, more suitable and even handsomer, to come to anything. Once you admit that you can change the object of a strongly-felt affection, you undermine the whole structure of love and marriage, the whole philosophy of Shakespeare's sonnet: this had been the approved, though unspoken, opinion of the rectory and its mental acres of upper air. Joanna pressed down her feelings for the second curate and worked them off in tennis and the war effort. She had not encouraged the second curate at all but brooded silently upon him until the Sunday she saw him standing in the pulpit and announce his sermon upon the text:

... if thy right eye offend thee, pluck it out, and cast it from thee: for it is profitable for thee that one of thy members should perish, and not that thy whole body should be cast into hell.

And if thy right hand offend thee, cut it off, and cast it from thee: for it is profitable for thee that one of thy members should perish, and not that thy whole body should be cast into hell.

It was the evening service. Many young girls from the district had come, some of them in their service uniforms. One particular Wren looked up at the curate, her pink cheeks touched by the stained-glass evening light; her hair curled lightly upwards on her Wren hat. Joanna could hardly imagine a more handsome man than this second curate. He was newly ordained, and was shortly going into the Air Force. It was spring, full of preparations and guesses, for the second front was to be established against the enemy, some said in North Africa, some said Scandinavia, the Baltic, France. Meantime, Joanna listened attentively to the young man in the pulpit, she listened obsessively. He was dark and tall, his eyes were deep under his straight black brows, he had a chiselled look. His wide mouth suggested to Joanna generosity and humour, that type of generosity and humour special to the bishop sprouting within him. He was very athletic. He had made it as clear that he wanted Joanna as the former curate had not. Like the rector's eldest daughter that she was, Joanna sat in her pew without seeming to listen in any particular way to this attractive fellow. She did not turn her face towards him as the pretty Wren was doing. The right eye and the right hand, he was saying, means that which we hold most precious. What the scripture meant, he said, was that if anything we hold most dear should prove an offence – as you know, he said, the Greek word here was *oxàvalov*, frequently occurring in Scripture in the connotation of scandal, offence, stumbling-block, as when St Paul said . . . The rustics who predominated in the congregation looked on with their round moveless eyes. Joanna decided to pluck out her right eye, cut off her right hand, this looming offence to the first love, this stumbling-block, the adorable man in the pulpit.

'For it is profitable for thee that one of thy members should perish, and not that thy whole body should be cast into hell,' rang the preacher's voice. 'Hell of course,' he said, 'is a negative concept. Let us put it more positively. More positively, the text should read, "It is better to enter maimed into the Kingdom of Heaven than not to enter at all."' He hoped to publish this sermon one day in a Collected Sermons, for he was as yet inexperienced in many respects, although he later learned some reality as an Air Force chaplain.

Joanna, then, had decided to enter maimed into the Kingdom of Heaven. By no means did she look maimed. She got a job in London and settled at the May of Teck Club. She took up elocution in her spare time. Then, towards the end of the war, she began to study and make a full-time occupation of it. The sensation of poetry replaced the sensation of the curate and she took on pupils at six shillings an hour pending her diploma.

> The wanton troopers riding by
> Have shot my fawn, and it will die.

Nobody at the May of Teck Club knew her precise history, but it was generally assumed to be something emotionally heroic. She was compared to Ingrid Bergman, and did not take part in the argument between members and staff about the food, whether it contained too many fattening properties, even allowing for the necessities of wartime rationing.

3

Love and money were the vital themes in all the bedrooms
and dormitories. Love came first, and subsidiary to it was
money for the upkeep of looks and the purchase of clothing
coupons at the official black-market price of eight coupons
for a pound.

The house was a spacious Victorian one, and very little
had been done to change its interior since the days when it
was a private residence. It resembled in its plan most of the
women's hostels, noted for cheapness and tone, which had
flourished since the emancipation of women had called for
them. No one at the May of Teck Club referred to it as a
hostel, except in moments of low personal morale such as
was experienced by the youngest members only on being
given the brush-off by a boy-friend.

The basement of the house was occupied by kitchens,
the laundry, the furnace and fuel-stores.

The ground floor contained staff offices, the dining-room,
the recreation room and, newly papered in a mud-like shade
of brown, the drawing-room. This resented wallpaper had
unfortunately been found at the back of a cupboard in huge
quantities, otherwise the walls would have remained grey
and stricken like everyone else's.

Boy-friends were allowed to dine as guests at a cost of
two-and-sixpence. It was also permitted to entertain in the
recreation room, on the terrace which led out from it, and

in the drawing-room whose mud-brown walls appeared so penitential in tone at that time – for the members were not to know that within a few years many of them would be lining the walls of their own homes with paper of a similar colour, it then having become smart.

Above this, on the first floor, where, in the former days of private wealth, an enormous ballroom had existed, an enormous dormitory now existed. This was curtained off into numerous cubicles. Here lived the very youngest members, girls between the ages of eighteen and twenty who had not long moved out of the cubicles of school dormitories throughout the English countryside, and who understood dormitory life from start to finish. The girls on this floor were not yet experienced in discussing men. Everything turned on whether the man in question was a good dancer and had a sense of humour. The Air Force was mostly favoured, and a D.F.C. was an asset. A Battle of Britain record aged a man in the eyes of the first-floor dormitory, in the year 1945. Dunkirk, too, was largely something that their fathers had done. It was the air heroes of the Normandy landing who were popular, lounging among the cushions in the drawing-room. They gave full entertainment value:

'Do you know the story of the two cats that went to Wimbledon? – Well, one cat persuaded another to go to Wimbledon to watch the tennis. After a few sets one cat said to the other, "I must say, I'm bloody bored. I honestly can't see why you're so interested in this game of tennis." And the other cat replied, "Well, my father's in the racquet!" '

'No!' shrieked the girls, and duly doubled up.

'But that's not the end of the story. There was a colonel sitting behind these two cats. He was watching the tennis because the war was on and so there wasn't anything for him to do. Well, this colonel had his dog with him. So when the cats started talking to each other the dog turned to the colonel and said, "Do you hear those two cats in front of us?" "No, shut up," said the colonel, "I'm concentrating on the game." "All right," said the dog – very happy this dog, you know – "I only thought you might be interested in a couple of cats that can talk." '

'Really,' said the voice of the dormitory later on, a twittering outburst, 'what a wizard sense of humour!' They were like birds waking up instead of girls going to bed, since 'Really, what a wizard sense of humour' would be the approximate collective euphony of the birds in the park five hours later, if anyone was listening.

On the floor above the dormitory were the rooms of the staff and the shared bedrooms of those who could afford shared bedrooms rather than a cubicle. Those who shared, four or two to a room, tended to be young women in transit, or temporary members looking for flats and bed-sitting rooms. Here, on the second floor, two of the elder spinsters, Collie and Jarvie, shared a room as they had done for eight years, since they were saving money now for their old age.

But on the floor above that, there seemed to have congregated, by instinctive consent, most of the celibates, the old maids of settled character and various ages, those who had decided on a spinster's life, and those who would one day do so but had not yet discerned the fact for themselves.

This third-floor landing had contained five large bedrooms, now partitioned by builders into ten small ones. The occupants ranged from prim and pretty young virgins who would never become fully-wakened women, to bossy ones in their late twenties who were too wide-awake ever to surrender to any man. Greggie, the third of the elder spinsters, had her room on this floor. She was the least prim and the kindest of the women there.

On this floor was the room of a mad girl, Pauline Fox, who was wont to dress carefully on certain evenings in the long dresses which were swiftly and temporarily reverted to in the years immediately following the war. She also wore long white gloves, and her hair was long, curling over her shoulders. On these evenings she said she was going to dine with the famous actor, Jack Buchanan. No one disbelieved her outright, and her madness was undetected.

Here, too, was Joanna Childe's room from which she could be heard practising her elocution at times when the recreation room was occupied.

> All the flowers of the spring
> Meet to perfume our burying;

At the top of the house, on the fourth floor, the most attractive, sophisticated and lively girls had their rooms. They were filled with deeper and deeper social longings of various kinds, as peace-time crept over everyone. Five girls occupied the five top rooms. Three of them had lovers in addition to men-friends with whom they did not sleep but whom they cultivated with a view to marriage. Of the remaining two, one was almost engaged to be married, and the other was Jane Wright, fat but intellectually glamorous by virtue of the fact that she worked for a publisher. She was on the look-out for a husband, meanwhile being mixed up with young intellectuals.

Nothing but the roof-tops lay above this floor, now inaccessible by the trap-door in the bathroom ceiling – a mere useless square since it had been bricked up long ago before the war after a girl had been attacked by a burglar or a lover who had entered by it – attacked or merely confronted unexpectedly, or found in bed with him as some said; as the case might be, he left behind him a legend of many screams in the night and the skylight had been henceforth closed to the public. Workmen who, from time to time, were called in to do something up above the house had to approach the roof from the attic of a neighbouring hotel. Greggie claimed to know all about the story, she knew everything about the club. Indeed it was Greggie who, inspired by a shaft of remembrance, had directed the warden to the hoard of mud-coloured wallpaper in the cupboard which now defiled the walls of the drawing-room and leered in the sunlight at everyone. The top-floor girls had often thought it might be a good idea to sunbathe on the flat portion of the roof and had climbed up on chairs to see about the opening of the trap-door. But it would not budge, and Greggie had once more told them why. Greggie produced a better version of the story every time.

'If there was a fire, we'd be stuck,' said Selina Redwood who was exceedingly beautiful.

'You've obviously been taking no notice of the emergency instructions,' Greggie said. This was true. Selina was seldom in to dinner and so she had never heard them. Four times a year the emergency instructions were read out by the warden after dinner, on which nights no guests were allowed. The top floor was served for emergency purposes by a back staircase leading down two flights to the perfectly sound fire-escape, and by the fire-equipment which lay around everywhere in the club. On these evenings of no guests the members were also reminded about putting things down lavatories, and the difficulties of plumbing systems in old houses, and of obtaining plumbers these days. They were reminded that they were expected to put everything back in place after a dance had been held in the club. Why some members unfortunately just went off to night clubs with their men-friends and left everything to others, said the warden, she simply did not know.

Selina had missed all this, never having been in to dinner on the warden's nights. From her window she could see, level with the top floor of the house, and set back behind the chimney pots, the portion of flat roof, shared by the club with the hotel next door, which would have been ideal for sunbathing. There was no access to any part of the roof from the bedroom windows, but one day she noticed that it was accessible from the lavatory window, a narrow slit made narrower by the fact that the wall in which it was set had been sub-divided at some point in the house's history when the wash-rooms had been put in. One had to climb upon the lavatory seat to see the roof. Selina measured the window. The aperture was seven inches wide by fourteen inches long. It opened casement-wise.

'I believe I could get through the lavatory window,' she said to Anne Baberton who occupied the room opposite hers.

'Why do you want to get through the lavatory window?' said Anne.

'It leads out to the roof. There's only a short jump from the window.'

Selina was extremely slim. The question of weight and measurement was very important on the top floor. The ability or otherwise to wriggle sideways through the lavatory window would be one of those tests that only went to prove the club's food policy to be unnecessarily fattening.

'Suicidal,' said Jane Wright who was miserable about her fatness and spent much of her time in eager dread of the next meal, and in making resolutions what to eat of it and what to leave, and in making counter-resolutions in view of the fact that her work at the publishers' was essentially mental, which meant that her brain had to be fed more than most people's.

22

Among the five top-floor members only Selina Redwood and Anne Baberton could manage to wriggle through the lavatory window, and Anne only managed it naked, having made her body slippery with margarine. After the first attempt, when she had twisted her ankle on the downward leap and grazed her skin on the return clamber, Anne said she would in future use her soap ration to facilitate the exit. Soap was as tightly rationed as margarine, but more precious, for margarine was fattening, anyway. Face cream was too expensive to waste on the window venture.

Jane Wright could not see why Anne was so concerned about her one inch and a half on the hips more than Selina's, since Anne was already slender and already fixed up for marriage. She stood on the lavatory seat and threw out Anne's faded green dressing-gown for her to drape round her slippery body and asked what it was like out there. The two other girls on the floor were away for the weekend on this occasion.

Anne and Selina were peeping over the edge of the flat roof at a point where Jane could not see them. They returned to report that they had looked down on the back garden where Greggie was holding her conducted tour of the premises for the benefit of two new members. She had been showing them the spot where the bomb had fallen and failed to go off, and had been removed by a bomb-squad, during which operation everyone had been obliged to leave the house. Greggie had also been showing them the spot where, in her opinion, an unexploded bomb still lay.

The girls got themselves back into the house.

'Greggie and her sensations': Jane felt she could scream. She added, 'Cheese pie for supper tonight, guess how many calories?'

The answer, when they looked up the chart, was roughly 350 calories. 'Followed by stewed cherries,' said Jane, ninety-four calories normal helping unless sweetened by saccharine, in which case sixty-four calories. We've had over a thousand calories today already. It's always the same on Sundays. The bread-and-butter pudding alone was –'

'I didn't eat the bread-and-butter pudding,' said Anne. 'Bread-and-butter pudding is suicidal.'

'I only eat a little bit of everything,' Selina said. 'I feel starved all the time, actually.'

'Well, I'm doing brain-work,' said Jane.

Anne was walking about the landing sponging off all the margarine. She said, 'I've had to use up soap and margarine as well.'

'I can't lend you any soap this month,' Selina said. Selina had a regular supply of soap from an American Army officer who got it from a source of many desirable things, called the P.X. But she was accumulating a hoard of it, and had stopped lending.

Anne said, 'I don't want your bloody soap. Just don't ask for the taffeta, that's all.'

By this she meant a Schiaparelli taffeta evening dress which had been given to her by a fabulously rich aunt, after one wearing. This marvellous dress, which caused a stir wherever it went, was shared by all the top floor on special occasions, excluding Jane whom it did not fit. For lending it out Anne got various returns, such as three clothing coupons or a half-used piece of soap.

Jane went back to her brain-work and shut the door with a definite click. She was rather tyrannous about her brain-work, and made a fuss about other people's wire-lesses on the landing, and about the petty-mindedness of these haggling bouts that took place with Anne when the taffeta dress was wanted to support the rising wave of long-dress parties.

'You can't wear it to the Milroy. It's been twice to the Milroy . . . it's been to Quaglino's, Selina wore it to Quags, it's getting known all over London.'

'But it looks altogether different on me, Anne. You can have a whole sheet of sweet-coupons.'

'I don't want your bloody sweet-coupons. I give all mine to my grandmother.'

Then Jane would put out her head. 'Stop being so petty-minded and stop screeching. I'm doing brain-work.'

Jane had one smart thing in her wardrobe, a black coat and skirt made out of her father's evening clothes. Very few dinner jackets in England remained in their original form after the war. But this looted outfit of Jane's was too large for anyone to borrow; she was thankful for that, at least. The exact nature of her brain-work was a mystery to the club because, when asked about it, she reeled off fast an explanation of extreme and alien detail about costing, printers, lists, manuscripts, galleys and contracts.

'Well, Jane, you ought to get paid for all that extra work you do.'

'The world of books is essentially disinterested,' Jane said. She always referred to the publishing business as 'The world of books'. She was always hard up, so presumably ill paid. It was because she had to be careful of her shillings for the meter which controlled the gas-fire in her room that she was unable, so she said, to go on a diet during the winter, since one had to keep warm as well as feed one's brain.

Jane received from the club, on account of her brain-work and job in publishing, a certain amount of respect which was socially offset by the arrival in the front hall, every week or so, of a pale, thin foreigner, decidedly in his thirties, with dandruff on his dark overcoat, who would ask in the office for Miss Jane Wright, always adding, 'I wish to see her privately, please.' Word also spread round from the office that many of Jane's incoming telephone calls were from this man.

'Is that the May of Teck Club?'

'Yes.'

'May I speak to Miss Wright privately, please?'

At one of these moments the secretary on duty said to him, 'All the members' calls are private. We don't listen in.'

'Good. I would know if you did, I wait for the click before I speak. Kindly remember.'

Jane had to apologise to the office for him. 'He's a foreigner. It's in connection with the world of books. It isn't my fault.'

But another and more presentable man from the world of books had lately put in an appearance for Jane. She had brought him into the drawing-room and introduced him to Selina, Anne, and the mad girl Pauline Fox who dressed up for Jack Buchanan on her lunatic evenings.

This man, Nicholas Farringdon, had been rather charming, though shy. 'He's thoughtful,' Jane said. 'We think him brilliant but he's still feeling his way in the world of books.'

'Is he something in publishing?'

'Not at the moment. He's still feeling his way. He's writing something.'

Jane's brain-work was of three kinds. First, and secretly, she wrote poetry of a strictly non-rational order, in which occurred, in about the proportion of cherries in a cherry-cake, certain words that she described as 'of a smouldering nature', such as loins and lovers, the root, the rose, the seawrack and the shroud. Secondly, also secretly, she wrote letters of a friendly tone but with a business intention, under the auspices of the pale foreigner. Thirdly, and more openly, she sometimes did a little work in her room which overlapped from her day's duties at the small publisher's office.

She was the only assistant at Huy Throvis-Mew Ltd. Huy Throvis-Mew was the owner of the firm, and Mrs Huy Throvis-Mew was down as a director on the letter heading. Huy Throvis-Mew's private name was George Johnson, or at least it had been so for some years, although a few very old friends called him Con and older friends called him Arthur or Jimmie. However, he was George in Jane's time, and she would do anything for George, her white-bearded employer. She parcelled up the books, took them to the post or delivered them, answered the telephone, made tea, minded the baby when George's wife, Tilly, wanted to go and queue for fish, entered the takings into ledgers, entered two different versions of the petty cash and office expenses into two sets of books, and generally did a small publisher's business. After a year George allowed her to do some of the detective work on new authors, which he was convinced was essential to the publishing trade, and to find out their financial circumstances and psychological weak points so that he could deal with them to a publisher's best advantage.

Like the habit of changing his name after a number of years, which he had done only in the hope that his luck would turn with it, this practice of George's was fairly innocent, in that he never really succeeded in discovering the whole truth about an author, or in profiting by his investigations at all. Still, it was his system, and its plot-formation gave him a zest for each day's work. Formerly George had done these basic investigations himself, but lately he had begun to think he might have more luck by leaving the new author to Jane. A consignment of books, on their way to George, had recently been seized at the port of Harwich and ordered to be burnt by the local magistrates on the grounds of obscenity, and George was feeling unlucky at this particular time.

Besides, it saved him all the expense and nervous exhaustion involved in the vigilant lunching with unpredictable writers, and feeling his way with them as to whether their paranoia exceeded his. It was better altogether to let them talk to Jane in a café, or bed, or wherever she went with them. It was nerve-racking enough to George to wait for her report. He fancied that many times in the past year she had saved him from paying out more ready money for a book than necessary – as when she had reported a dire need for ready cash, or when she had told George exactly what part of the manuscript he should find fault with – it was usually the part in which the author took a special pride – in order to achieve the minimum resistance, if not the total collapse, of the author.

George had obtained a succession of three young wives on account of his continuous eloquence to them on the subject of the world of books, which they felt was an elevating one – he had deserted the other two, not they him – and he had not yet been declared bankrupt although he had undergone in the course of the years various tangled forms of business reconstruction which were probably too much for the nerves of his creditors to face legally, since none ever did.

George took a keen interest in Jane's training in the handling of a writer of books. Unlike his fireside eloquence to his wife Tilly, his advice to Jane in the office was furtive, for he half believed, in the twilight portion of his mind, that authors were sly enough to make themselves invisible and be always floating under the chairs of publishers' offices.

'You see, Jane,' said George, 'these tactics of mine are an essential part of the profession. All the publishers do it. The big firms do it too, they do it automatically. The big fellows can afford to do it automatically, they can't afford to acknowledge all the facts like me, too much face to lose. I've had to work out every move for myself and get everything clear in my mind where authors are concerned. In publishing, one is dealing with a temperamental raw material.'

He went over to the corner curtain which concealed a coat-rail, and pulled aside the curtain. He peered within, then closed the curtain again and continued, 'Always think of authors as your raw material, Jane, if you're going to stay in the world of books.' Jane took this for fact. She had now been given Nicholas Farringdon to work on. George had said he was a terrible risk. Jane judged his age to be just over thirty. He was known only as a poet of small talent and an anarchist of dubious loyalty to that cause; but even these details were not at first known to Jane. He had brought to George a worn-out-looking sheaf of typewritten pages, untidily stacked in a brown folder. The whole was entitled *The Sabbath Notebooks*.

Nicholas Farringdon differed in some noticeable respects from the other writers she had come across. He differed, unnoticeably so far, in that he knew he was being worked on. But meantime she observed he was more arrogant and more impatient than other authors of the intellectual class. She noticed he was more attractive.

She had achieved some success with the very intellectual author of *The Symbolism of Louisa May Alcott*, which George was now selling very well and fast in certain quarters, since it had a big lesbian theme. She had achieved some success with Rudi Bittesch, the Rumanian who called on her frequently at the club.

But Nicholas had produced a more upsetting effect than usual on George, who was moreover torn between his attraction to a book he could not understand and his fear of its failure. George handed him over to Jane for treatment and meanwhile complained nightly to Tilly that he was in the hands of a writer, lazy, irresponsible, insufferable and cunning.

Inspired by a brain-wave, Jane's first approach to a writer had been, 'What is your raison d'être?' It had worked marvellously. She tried it on Nicholas Farringdon when he called to the office about his manuscript one day when George was 'at a meeting', which was to say, hiding in the back office. 'What is your raison d'être, Mr Farringdon?'

He frowned at her in an abstract sort of way, as if she were a speaking machine that had gone wrong.

Inspired by another brain-wave Jane invited him to dine at the May of Teck Club. He accepted with a special modesty, plainly from concern for his book. It had been rejected by ten publishers already, as had most of the books that came to George.

His visit put Jane up in the estimation of the club. She had not expected him to react so eagerly to everything. Sipping black Nescafé in the drawing-room with Jane, Selina, dark little Judy Redwood and Anne, he had looked round with a faint, contented smile. Jane had chosen her companions for the evening with the instinct of an experimental procuress which, when she perceived the extent of its success, she partly regretted and partly congratulated herself on, since she had not been sure from various reports whether Nicholas preferred men, and now she concluded that he at least liked both sexes. Selina's long unsurpassable legs arranged themselves diagonally from the deep chair where she lolled in the distinct attitude of being the only woman present who could afford to loll. There was something about Selina's lolling which gave her a queenly eminence. She visibly appraised Nicholas, while he continued to glance here and there at the several groups of chattering girls in other parts of the room. The terrace doors stood wide open to the cool night and presently from the recreation room there came, by way of the terrace, the sound of Joanna in the process of an elocution lesson.

> I thought of Chatterton, the marvellous Boy,
> The sleepless Soul that perished in his pride;
> Of Him who walked in glory and in joy
> Following his plough, along the mountain-side;
> By our own spirits are we deified:
> We Poets in our youth begin in gladness;
> But thereof come in the end despondency and madness.

'I wish she would stick to *The Wreck of the Deutschland*,' Judy Redwood said. 'She's marvellous with Hopkins.'

Joanna's voice was saying, 'Remember the stress on Chatterton and the slight pause to follow.'

Joanna's pupil recited:

> I thought of Chatterton, the marvellous Boy,

The excitement over the slit window went on for the rest of the afternoon. Jane's brain-work proceeded against the background echoes of voices from the large wash-room where the lavatories were. The two other occupants of the top floor had returned, having been to their homes in the country for the weekend: Dorothy Markham, the impoverished niece of Lady Julia Markham who was chairwoman of the club's management committee, and Nancy Riddle, one of the club's many clergymen's daughters. Nancy was trying to overcome her Midlands accent, and took lessons in elocution from Joanna with this end in view.

31

Jane, at her brain-work, heard from the direction of the wash-room the success of Dorothy Markham's climb through the window. Dorothy's hips were thirty-six and a half inches; her bust measurement was only thirty-one, a fact which did not dismay her, as she intended to marry one of three young men out of her extensive acquaintance who happened to find themselves drawn to boyish figures, and although she did not know about such things as precisely as did her aunt, Dorothy knew well enough that her hipless and breastless shape would always attract the sort of young man who felt at home with it. Dorothy could emit, at any hour of the day or night, a waterfall of débutante chatter, which rightly gave the impression that on any occasion between talking, eating and sleeping, she did not think, except in terms of these phrase-ripples of hers: 'Filthy lunch.' 'The most gorgeous wedding.' 'He actually raped her, she was amazed.' 'Ghastly film.' 'I'm desperately well, thanks, how are you?'

Her voice from the wash-room distracted Jane: 'Oh hell, I'm black with soot, I'm absolutely filthington.' She opened Jane's door without knocking and put in her head. 'Got any soapyjo?' It was some months before she was to put her head round Jane's door and announce, 'Filthy luck. I'm preggers. Come to the wedding.'

Jane said, on being asked for the use of her soap, 'Can you lend me fifteen shillings till next Friday?' It was her final resort for getting rid of people when she was doing brain-work.

Evidently, from the sound of things, Nancy Riddle was stuck in the window. Nancy was getting hysterical. Finally, Nancy was released and calmed, as was betokened by the gradual replacement of Midlands vowels with standard English ones issuing from the wash-room.

Jane continued with her work, describing her effort to herself as pressing on regardless. All the club, infected by the Air Force idiom current amongst the dormitory virgins, used this phrase continually.

She had put aside Nicholas's manuscript for the time being, as it was a sticky proposition; she had not yet, in fact, grasped the theme of the book, as was necessary before deciding on a significant passage to cast doubt upon, although she had already thought of the comment she would recommend George to make: 'Don't you think this part is a bit derivative?' Jane had thought of it in a brain-wave.

She had put the book aside. She was at work, now, on some serious spare-time work for which she was paid. This came into the department of her life that had to do with Rudi Bittesch whom she hated, at this stage in her life, for his unattractive appearance. He was too old for her, besides everything else. When in a depressed state of mind, she found it useful to remember that she was only twenty-two, for the fact cheered her up. She looked down Rudi's list of famous authors and their respective addresses to see who still remained to be done. She took a sheet of writing paper and wrote her great-aunt's address in the country, followed by the date. She then wrote:

Dear Mr Hemingway,
     I am addressing this letter to you care of your publisher
in the confidence that it will be sent on to you.

This was an advisable preliminary, Rudi said, because sometimes publishers were instructed to open authors' letters and throw them away if not of sufficient business importance, but this approach, if it got into the publishers' hands, 'might touch their heart'. The rest of the letter was entirely Jane's province. She paused to await a small brain-wave, and after a moment continued:

I am sure you receive many admiring letters, and have hesitated to add yet another to your post-bag. But since my release from prison, where I have been for the past two years and four months, I have felt more and more that I want you to know how much your novels meant to me during that time. I had few visitors. My allotted weekly hours of leisure were spent in the Library. It was unheated alas, but I did not notice the cold as I read on. Nothing I read gave me so much courage to face the future and to build a new future on my release as *For Whom the Bell Tolls*. The novel gave me back my faith in life.

I just want you to know this, and to say 'Thank you'.

Yours sincerely

(Miss) J. Wright.

P.S. This is not a begging letter. I assure you I would return any money that was sent to me.

If this succeeded in reaching him it might bring a hand-written reply. The prison letter and the asylum letter were more liable to bring replies in the author's own hand than any other type of letter, but one had to choose an author 'with heart', as Rudi said. Authors without heart seldom replied at all, and if they did it was a type-written letter. For a type-written letter signed by the author, Rudi paid two shillings if the autograph was scarce, but if the author's signature was available everywhere, and the letter a mere formal acknowledgement, Rudi paid nothing. For a letter in the author's own hand-writing Rudi paid five shillings for the first page and a shilling thereafter. Jane's ingenuity was therefore awakened to the feat of composing the sort of letters which would best move the recipient to reply in total holograph.

Rudi paid for the writing paper and the postage. He told her he only wanted the letters 'for sentimental purpose of my collection'. She had seen his collection. But she assumed that he was collecting them with an eye to their increasing value year by year.

'If I write myself it does not ring true; I do not get interesting replies. By the way, my English is not like the English of an English girl.'

She would have made her own collection if only she had not needed the ready money, and could afford to save up the letters for the future.

'Never ask for money in your letters,' Rudi had warned her. 'Do not mention the subject of money. It makes criminal offence under false pretences.' However, she had the brain-wave of adding her postscript, to make sure.

Jane had worried, at first, lest she should be found out and get into some sort of trouble. Rudi reassured her. 'You say you only make a joke. It is not criminal. Who would check up on you, by the way? Do you think Bernard Shaw is going to write and make questions about you from the old aunt? Bernard Shaw is a Name.'

Bernard Shaw had in fact proved disappointing. He had sent a type-written postcard:

Thank you for your letter in praise of my writings. As you say they have consoled you in your misfortunes, I shall not attempt to gild the lily by my personal comments. As you say you desire no money I shall not press upon you my holograph signature which has some cash value. G.B.S.

The initials, too, had been typed.

Jane learned by experience. Her illegitimate-child letter brought a sympathetic reply from Daphne du Maurier, for which Rudi paid his price. With some authors a scholarly question about the underlying meaning worked best. One

35

day, on a brain-wave, she wrote to Henry James at the Athenaeum Club.

'That was foolish of you because James is dead, by the way,' Rudi said.

'Do you want a letter from an author called Nicholas Farringdon?' she said.

'No, I have known Nicholas Farringdon, he's no good, he is not likely to be a Name ever. What has he written?'

'A book called *The Sabbath Notebooks*.'

'Is it religious?'

'Well, he calls it political philosophy. It's just a lot of notes and thoughts.'

'It smells religious. He will finish up as a reactionary Catholic, to obey the Pope. Already I have predicted this before the war.'

'He's jolly good-looking.'

She hated Rudi. He was not at all attractive. She addressed and stamped her letter to Ernest Hemingway and ticked off his name on the list, writing the date beside it. The girls' voices had disappeared from the wash-room. Anne's wireless was singing:

> There were angels dining at the Ritz
> And a nightingale sang in Berkeley Square.

It was twenty minutes past six. There was time for one more letter before supper. Jane looked down the list.

Dear Mr Maugham,
    I am addressing this letter to you at your club . . .

Jane paused for thought. She ate a square of chocolate to keep her brain going till supper-time. The prison letter might not appeal to Maugham. Rudi had said he was cynical about human nature. On a brain-wave she recalled that he had been a doctor. It might be an idea to make up a sanatorium letter . . . She had been ill for two years and four months with tuberculosis. After all, this disease was not attributable to human nature, there was nothing in it to be cynical about. She regretted having eaten the chocolate, and put the rest of the bar right at the back of a shelf in her cupboard where it was difficult to reach, as if hiding it from a child. The rightness of this action and the wrongness of her having eaten any at all were confirmed by Selina's voice from Anne's room. Anne had turned off the wireless and they had been talking. Selina would probably be stretched out on Anne's bed in her languid manner. This became certain as Selina began to repeat, slowly and solemnly, the Two Sentences.

The Two Sentences were a simple morning and evening exercise prescribed by the Chief Instructress of the Poise Course which Selina had recently taken, by correspondence, in twelve lessons for five guineas. The Poise Course believed strongly in auto-suggestion and had advised, for the maintenance of poise in the working woman, a repetition of the following two sentences twice a day:

> Poise is perfect balance, an equanimity of body and mind, complete composure whatever the social scene. Elegant dress, immaculate grooming, and perfect deportment all contribute to the attainment of self-confidence.

Even Dorothy Markham stopped her chatter for a few seconds every morning at eight-thirty and evening at six-thirty, in respect for Selina's Sentences. All the top floor was respectful. It had cost five guineas. The two floors below were indifferent. But the dormitories crept up on the landings to listen, they could hardly believe their ears, and saved up each word with savage joy to make their boy-friends in the Air Force laugh like a drain, which was how laughter was described in those circles. At the same time, the dormitory girls were envious of Selina, knowing in their hearts they would never quite be in the Selina class where looks were concerned.

The Sentences were finished by the time Jane had shoved her remaining piece of chocolate well out of sight and range. She returned to the letter. She had T.B. She gave a frail cough and looked round the room. It contained a wash-basin, a bed, a chest-of-drawers, a cupboard, a table and lamp, a wicker chair, a hard chair, a bookcase, a gas-fire and a meter-box with a slot to measure the gas, shilling by shilling. Jane felt she might easily be in a room in a sanatorium.

'One last time,' said Joanna's voice from the floor below. She was now rehearsing Nancy Riddle, who was at this moment managing her standard English vowels very well.

'And again,' said Joanna. 'We've just got time before supper. I'll read the first stanza, then you follow on.'

> At the top of the house the apples are laid in rows,
> And the skylight lets the moonlight in, and those
> Apples are deep-sea apples of green. There goes
> A cloud on the moon in the autumn night.

4

It was July 1945, three weeks before the general election.

> They are lying in rows there, under the gloomy beams;
> On the sagging floor; they gather the silver streams
> Out of the moon, those moonlit apples of dreams
>   And quiet is the steep stair under.

'I wish she would stick to *The Wreck of the Deutschland*.'
  'Do you? I rather like *Moonlit Apples*.'

We come now to Nicholas Farringdon in his thirty-third year. He was said to be an anarchist. No one at the May of Teck Club took this seriously as he looked quite normal; that is to say, he looked slightly dissipated, like the disappointing son of a good English family that he was. That each of his brothers – two accountants and one dentist – said of him from the time he left Cambridge in the mid 1930s, 'Nicholas is a bit of a misfit, I'm afraid,' would not have surprised anyone.

Jane Wright applied for information about him to Rudi Bittesch who had known Nicholas throughout the 1930s. 'You don't bother with him. He is a mess by the way,' Rudi said. 'I know him well, he is a good friend of mine.' From Rudi she gathered that before the war he had been always undecided whether to live in England or France, and whether he preferred men or women, since he alternated between passionate intervals with both. Also, he could never make up his mind between suicide and an equally drastic course of action known as Father D'Arcy. Rudi explained that the latter was a Jesuit philosopher who had the monopoly for converting the English intellectuals. Nicholas was a pacifist up to the outbreak of war, Rudi said, then he joined the Army. Rudi said, 'I have met him one day in Piccadilly wearing his uniform, and he said to me the war has brought him peace. Next thing he is psychoanalysed out of the Army, a wangle, and he is working for the Intelligence. The anarchists have given him up but he calls himself an anarchist, by the way.'

Far from putting Jane against Nicholas Farringdon, the scraps of his history that came to her by way of Rudi gave him an irresistible heroism in her mind, and, through her, in the eyes of the top-floor girls.

'He must be a genius,' said Nancy Riddle.

Nicholas had a habit of saying 'When I'm famous . . .' when referring to the remote future, with the same cheerful irony that went into the preface of the bus conductor on the No. 73 route to his comments on the law of the land: 'When I come to power . . .'

Jane showed Rudi *The Sabbath Notebooks*, so entitled because Nicholas had used as an epigraph the text 'The Sabbath was made for Man, not Man for the Sabbath'.

'George must be out of his mind to publish this,' Rudi said when he brought it back to Jane. They sat in the recreation room at the other end of which, cornerwise by the open French window, a girl was practising scales on the piano with as much style as she could decently apply to the scales. The music-box tinkle was far enough away, and sufficiently dispersed by the Sunday morning sounds from the terrace, not to intrude too strongly on Rudi's voice, as he read out, in his foreign English, small passages from Nicholas's book in order to prove something to Jane. He did this as a cloth merchant, perhaps wishing to persuade a customer to buy his best quality of goods, might first produce samples of inferior stuff, feel it, invite comment, shrug, and toss it away. Jane was convinced that Rudi was right in his judgement of what he was reading, but she was really more fascinated by what small glimpses of Nicholas Farringdon's personality she got from Rudi's passing remarks. Nicholas was the only presentable intellectual she had met.

'It is not bad, not good,' said Rudi, putting his head this way, that way, as he said it. 'It is mediocrity. I recall he composed this in nineteen thirty-eight when he had a freck-led bed-mate of the female sex; she was an anarchist and pacifist. Listen, by the way . . .' He read out:

X is writing a history of anarchism. Anarchism properly has no history in the sense that X intends – i.e. in the sense of continuity and development. It is a spontaneous move-ment of people in particular times and circumstances. A history of anarchism would not be in the nature of political history, it would be analogous to a history of the heart-beat. One may make new discoveries about it, one may compare its reactions under varying conditions, but there is nothing new of itself.

Jane was thinking of the freckled girl-friend whom Nicholas had slept with at the time, and she almost fancied they had taken *The Sabbath Notebooks* to bed together. 'What happened to his girl-friend?' Jane said. 'There is nothing wrong with this,' Rudi said, referring to what he had just read, 'but it is not so magnificent a great truth that he should like a great man place it on the page, by the way, in a paragraph alone. He makes *pensées* as he is too lazy to write the essay. Listen . . .'

Jane said, 'What happened to the girl?'

'She went to prison for pacifism maybe, I don't know. If I would be George I would not touch this book. Listen . . .'

Every communist has a fascist frown; every fascist has a communist smile.

'Ha!' said Rudi.

'I thought that was a very profound bit,' Jane said, as it was the only bit she could remember.

'That is why he writes it in, he counts that the bloody book has got to have a public, so he puts in some little bit of aphorism, very clever, that a girl like you likes to hear, by the way. It means nothing, this, where is the meaning?' Most of Rudi's last words were louder-sounding than he had intended, as the girl at the piano had paused for rest.

'There's no need to get excited,' said Jane loudly.

The girl at the piano started a new set of rippling tinkles.

'We move to the drawing-room,' said Rudi.

'No, everyone's in the drawing-room this morning,' Jane said. 'There's not a quiet corner in the drawing-room.' She did not particularly want to display Rudi to the rest of the club.

Up and down the scales went the girl at the piano. From a window above, Joanna, fitting in an elocution lesson with Miss Harper, the cook, in the half-hour before the Sunday joint was ready to go in the oven, said, 'Listen':

> Ah! Sun-flower! weary of time,
> Who countest the steps of the Sun;
> Seeking after that sweet golden clime,
> Where the traveller's journey is done;

42

'Now try it,' said Joanna. 'Very slowly on the third line. Think of a sweet golden clime as you say it.'

Ah! Sun-flower! . . .

The dormitory girls who had spilled out of the drawing-room on to the terrace chattered like a parliament of fowls. The little notes of the scales followed one another obediently. 'Listen,' said Rudi:

> Everyone should be persuaded to remember how far, and
> with what a pathetic thump, the world has fallen from grace,
> that it needs must appoint politicians for its keepers, that
> its emotions, whether of consolation at breakfast-time or
> fear in the evening . . .

Rudi said, 'You notice his words, that he says the world has fallen from grace? This is the reason that he is no anarchist, by the way. They chuck him out when he talks like a son of the Pope. This man is a mess that he calls himself an anarchist; the anarchists do not make all that talk of original sin, so forth; they permit only anti-social tendencies, unethical conduct, so forth. Nick Farringdon is a diversionist, by the way.'

'Do you call him Nick?' Jane said.

'Sometimes in the pubs, the Wheatsheaf and the Gargoyle, so on, he was Nick in those days. Except there was a barrow-boy called him Mr Farringdon. Nicholas said to him, "Look, I wasn't christened Mister," but was no good; the barrow-boy was his friend, by the way.'

'Once more,' said Joanna's voice.

Ah! Sun-flower! weary of time,

'Listen,' said Rudi:

Nevertheless, let our moment or opportunity be stated. We do not need a government. We do not need a House of Commons. Parliament should dissolve forever. We could manage very well in our movement towards a complete anarchist society, with our great but powerless institutions: we could manage with the monarchy as an example of the dignity inherent in the free giving and receiving of precedence and favour without power; the churches for the spiritual needs of the people; the House of Lords for purposes of debate and recommendation; and the universities for consultation. We do not need institutions with power. The practical affairs of society could be dealt with locally by the Town, Borough, and Village Councils. International affairs could be conducted by variable representatives in a non-professional capacity. We do not need professional politicians with an eye to power. The grocer, the doctor, the cook, should serve their country for a term as men serve on a jury. We can be ruled by the corporate will of men's hearts alone. It is Power that is defunct, not as we are taught, the powerless institutions.

'I ask you a question,' Rudi said. 'It is a simple question. He wants monarchy, he wants anarchism. What does he want? These two are enemies in all of history. Simple answer is, he is a mess.'

'How old was the barrow-boy?' Jane said.

'And again,' said Joanna's voice from the upper window.

Dorothy Markham had joined the girls on the sunny terrace. She was telling a hunting story. '. . . the only one time I've been thrown it shook me to the core. What a brute!'

'Where did you land?'

'Where do you think?'

The girl at the piano stopped and folded her scale-sheet with seemly concentration.

'I go,' said Rudi, looking at his watch. 'I have an appointment to meet a contact for a drink.' He rose and once more, before he handed over the book, flicked through the type-written pages. He said, sadly, 'Nicholas is a friend of mine, but I regret to say he's a non-contributive thinker, by the way. Come here, listen to this.'

There is a kind of truth in the popular idea of an anarchist as a wild man with a home-made bomb in his pocket. In modern times this bomb, fabricated in the back workshops of the imagination, can only take one effective form: Ridicule.

Jane said, ' "Only take" isn't grammatical, it should be "take only". I'll have to change that, Rudi.'

So much for the portrait of the martyr as a young man as it was suggested to Jane on a Sunday morning between armistice and armistice, in the days of everyone's poverty, in 1945. Jane, who lived to distort it in many elaborate forms, at the time merely felt she was in touch with something reckless, intellectual, and Bohemian by being in touch with Nicholas. Rudi's contemptuous attitude bounded back upon himself in her estimation. She felt she knew too much about Rudi to respect him; and was presently astonished to find that there was indeed a sort of friendship between himself and Nicholas, lingering on from the past.

Meantime, Nicholas touched lightly on the imagination of the girls of slender means, and they on his. He had not yet slept on the roof with Selina on the hot summer nights – he gaining access from the American-occupied attic of the

45

hotel next door, and she through the slit window – and he had not yet witnessed that action of savagery so extreme that it forced him involuntarily to make an entirely unaccustomed gesture, the signing of the cross upon himself. At this time Nicholas still worked for one of those left-hand departments of the Foreign Office, the doings of which the right-hand did not know. It came under Intelligence. After the Normandy landing he had been sent on several missions to France. Now there was very little left for his department to do except wind-up. Winding-up was arduous, it involved the shuffling of papers and people from office to office; particularly it involved considerable shuffling between the British and American Intelligence pockets in London. He had a bleak furnished room at Fulham. He was bored.

'I've got something to tell you, Rudi,' said Jane.

'Hold on, please, I have a customer.'

'I'll ring you back later, then, I'm in a hurry. I only wanted to tell you that Nicholas Farringdon's dead. Remember that book of his he never published – he gave you the manuscript. Well, it might be worth something now, and I thought –'

'Nick's dead? Hold on, please, Jane. I have a customer waiting here to buy a book. Hold on.'

'I'll ring you later.'

Nicholas came, then, to dine at the club.

> I thought of Chatterton, the marvellous Boy,
> The sleepless Soul that perished in his Pride;

'Who is that?'

'It's Joanna Childe, she teaches elocution, you must meet her.'

The twittering movements at other points in the room, Joanna's singular voice, the beautiful aspects of poverty and charm amongst these girls in the brown-papered drawing-room, Selina, furled like a long soft sash, in her chair, came to Nicholas in a gratuitous flow. Months of boredom had subdued him to intoxication by an experience which, at another time, might itself have bored him.

Some days later he took Jane to a party to meet the people she longed to meet, young male poets in corduroy trousers and young female poets with waist-length hair, or at least females who typed the poetry and slept with the poets, it was nearly the same thing. Nicholas took her to supper at Bertorelli's; then he took her to a poetry reading at a hired meeting-house in the Fulham Road; then he took her on to a party with some of the people he had collected from the reading. One of the poets who was well thought of had acquired a job at Associated News in Fleet Street, in honour of which he had purchased a pair of luxurious pigskin gloves; he displayed these proudly. There was an air of a resistance movement against the world at this poetry meeting. Poets seemed to understand each other with a secret instinct, almost a kind of prearrangement, and it was plain that the poet with the gloves would never show off these poetic gloves so frankly, or expect to be understood so well in relation to them, at his new job in Fleet Street or anywhere else, as here.

Some were men demobilised from the non-combatant corps. Some had been unfit for service for obvious reasons – a nervous twitch of the facial muscles, bad eyesight, or a limp. Others were still in battle dress. Nicholas had been out of the Army since the month after Dunkirk, from which he had escaped with a wound in the thumb; his release from the army had followed a mild nervous disorder in the month after Dunkirk.

Nicholas stood noticeably aloof at the poets' gathering, but although he greeted his friends with a decided reserve, it was evident that he wanted Jane to savour her full joy of it. In fact, he wanted her to invite him again to the May of Teck Club, as dawned on her later in the evening.

The poets read their poems, two each, and were applauded. Some of these poets were to fail and fade into a no-man's-land of Soho public houses in a few years' time, and become the familiar messes of literary life. Some, with many talents, faltered, in time, from lack of stamina, gave up and took a job in advertising or publishing, detesting literary people above all. Others succeeded and became paradoxes; they did not always continue to write poetry, or even poetry exclusively.

One of these young poets, Ernest Claymore, later became a mystical stockbroker of the 1960s, spending his weekdays urgently in the City, three weekends each month at his country cottage – an establishment of fourteen rooms, where he ignored his wife and, alone in his study, wrote Thought – and one weekend a month in retreat at a monastery. In the 1960s Ernest Claymore read a book a week in bed before sleep, and sometimes addressed a letter to the press about a book review: 'Sir, Maybe I'm dim. I have read your review of . . .'; he was to publish three short books of philosophy which everyone could easily understand indeed; at the moment in question, the summer of 1945, he was a dark-eyed young poet at the poetry recital, and had just finished reading, with husky force, his second contribution:

> I in my troubled night of the dove clove brightly my Path
> from the tomb of love incessantly to redress my Articulate
> womb, that new and necessary rose, exposing my . . .

He belonged to the Cosmic school of poets. Jane, perceiving that he was orthosexual by definition of his manner and appearance, was uncertain whether to cultivate him for future acquaintance or whether to hang on to Nicholas. She managed to do both, since Nicholas brought along this dark husky poet, this stockbroker to be, to the party which followed, and there Jane was able to make a future assignment with him before Nicholas drew her aside to inquire further into the mysterious life of the May of Teck Club.

'It's just a girls' hostel,' she said, 'that's all it boils down to.'

Beer was served in jam-jars, which was an affectation of the highest order, since jam-jars were at that time in shorter supply than glasses and mugs. The house where the party was held was in Hampstead. There was a stifling crowd. The hosts, Nicholas said, were communist intellectuals. He led her up to a bedroom where they sat on the edge of an unmade bed and looked, with philosophical exhaustion on Nicholas's side, and on hers the enthusiasm of the neophyte Bohemian, at the bare boards of the floor. The people of the house, said Nicholas, were undeniably communist intellectuals, as one could see from the variety of dyspepsia remedies on the bathroom shelf. He said he would point them out to her on the way downstairs when they rejoined the party. By no means, said Nicholas, did the hosts expect to meet their guests at this party. 'Tell me about Selina,' said Nicholas.

Jane's dark hair was piled on top of her head. She had a large face. The only attractive thing about her was her youth and those mental areas of inexperience she was not yet conscious of. She had forgotten for the time being that her job was to reduce Nicholas's literary morale as far as possible, and was treacherously behaving as if he were the genius that, before the week was out, he claimed to be in the letter he got her to forge for him in Charles Morgan's name.

Nicholas had decided to do everything nice for Jane, except sleep with her, in the interests of two projects: the publication of his book and his infiltration of the May of Teck Club in general and Selina in particular. 'Tell me more about Selina.' Jane did not then, or at any time, realise that he had received from his first visit to the May of Teck Club a poetic image that teased his mind and pestered him for details as he now pestered Jane. She knew nothing of his boredom and social discontent. She did not see the May of Teck Club as a microcosmic ideal society; far from it. The beautiful heedless poverty of a Golden Age did not come into the shilling meter life which any sane girl would regard only as a temporary one until better opportunities occurred.

> A damsel with a dulcimer
> In a vision once I saw:
> It was an Abyssinian maid,

The voice had wafted with the night breeze into the drawing-room. Nicholas said, now, 'Tell me about the elocution teacher.'

'Oh, Joanna – you must meet her.'

'Tell me about the borrowing and lending of clothes.'

Jane pondered as to what she could barter for this information which he seemed to want. The party downstairs was going on without them. The bare boards under her feet and the patchy walls seemed to hold out no promise of becoming memorable by tomorrow. She said, 'We've got to discuss your book some time. George and I've got a list of queries.'

Nicholas lolled on the unmade bed and casually thought he would probably have to plan some defence measures with George. His jam-jar was empty. He said, 'Tell me more about Selina. What does she do apart from being secretary to a pansy?'

Jane was not sure how drunk she was, and could not bring herself to stand up, this being the test. She said, 'Come to lunch on Sunday.' Sunday lunch for a guest was two-and-six-pence extra; she felt she might be taken to more of these parties by Nicholas, among the inner circle of the poets of today; but she supposed he wanted to take Selina out, and that was that; she thought he would probably want to sleep with Selina, and as Selina had slept with two men already, Jane did not envisage any obstacle. It made her sad to think, as she did, that the whole rigmarole of his interest in the May of Teck Club, and the point of their sitting in this bleak room, was his desire to sleep with Selina. She said, 'What bits would you say were the most important?'

'What bits?'

'Your book,' she said. '*The Sabbath Notebooks*. George is looking for a genius. It must be you.'

'It's all important.' He formed the plan immediately of forging a letter from someone crudely famous to say it was a work of genius. Not that he believed it to be one way or the other, the idea of such an unspecific attribute as genius not being one on which his mind was accustomed to waste its time. However, he knew a useful word when he saw it, and perceiving the trend of Jane's question, made his plan. He said, 'Tell me again that delightful thing Selina repeats about poise.'

'Poise is perfect balance, an equanimity of body and mind, complete composure whatever the social scene. Elegant dress, immaculate ... Oh, Christ,' she said, 'I'm tired of picking crumbs of meat out of the shepherd's pie, picking with a fork to get the little bits of meat separated from the little bits of potato. You don't know what it's like trying to eat enough to live on and at the same time avoid fats and carbohydrates.'

Nicholas kissed her tenderly. He felt there might be a sweetness in Jane, after all, for nothing reveals a secret sweetness so much as a personal point of misery bursting out of a phlegmatic creature.

Jane said, 'I've got to feed my brain.'

He said he would try to get her a pair of nylon stockings from the American with whom he worked. Her legs were bare and dark-haired. There and then he gave her six clothing coupons out of his coupon book. He said she could have his next week's egg. She said, 'You need your egg for your brain.'

'I have breakfast at the American canteen,' he said. 'We have eggs there, and orange juice.'

She said she would take his egg. The egg-ration was one a week at this time, it was the beginning of the hardest period of food-rationing, since the liberated countries had now to be supplied. Nicholas had a gas-ring in his bed-sitting room on which he cooked his supper when he was at home and remembered about supper. He said, 'You can have all my tea, I drink coffee. I get it from the Americans.'

She said she would be glad of his tea. The tea-ration was two ounces one week and three ounces the next, alternately. Tea was useful for bartering purposes. She felt she would really have to take the author's side, where Nicholas was concerned, and somehow hoodwink George. Nicholas was a true artist and had some feelings. George was only a publisher. She would have to put Nicholas wise to George's fault-finding technique of business.

'Let's go down,' Nicholas said.

The door opened and Rudi Bittesch stood watching them for a moment. Rudi was always sober.

'Rudi!' said Jane with unusual enthusiasm. She was glad to be seen to know somebody in this milieu who had not been introduced by Nicholas. It was a way of showing that she belonged to it.

'Well, well,' Rudi said. 'How are you doing these days, Nick, by the way?'

Nicholas said he was on loan to the Americans.

Rudi laughed like a cynical uncle and said, himself he too could have worked for the Americans if he had wanted to sell out.

'Sell out what?' Nicholas said.

'My integrity to work only for peace,' said Rudi. 'By the way, come and join the party and forget it.'

On the way down he said to Nicholas, 'You're publishing a book with Throvis-Mew? I hear this news by Jane.'

Jane said quickly, in case Rudi should reveal that he had already seen the book, 'It's a sort of anarchist book.'

Rudi said to Nicholas, 'You still like anarchism, by the way?'

'But not anarchists by and large, by the way,' Nicholas said.

'How has he died, by the way?' said Rudi.

'He was martyred, they say,' said Jane.

'In Haiti? How is this?'

'I don't know much, except what I get from the news sources. Reuters says a local rising. Associated News has a bit that's just come in . . . I was thinking of that manuscript *The Sabbath Notebooks*.'

'I have it still. If he is famous by his death, I find it. How has he died . . . ?'

'I can't hear you, it's a rotten line . . . I say I can't hear, Rudi . . .'

'How has he died . . . By what means?'

'It will be worth a lot of money, Rudi.'

'I find it. This line is bad by the way, can you hear me? How has he died . . . ?'

'. . . a hut . . .'

'I can't hear . . .'

'. . . in a valley . . .'

'Speak loud.'

'. . . in a clump of palms . . . deserted . . . it was market day, everyone had gone to market.'

'I find it. There is maybe a market for this Sabbath book. They make a cult of him, by the way?'

'He was trying to interfere with their superstitions, they said. They're getting rid of a lot of Catholic priests.'

'I can't hear a word. I ring you tonight, Jane. We meet later.'

5

Selina came into the drawing-room wearing a high hoop-brimmed blue hat and shoes with high block wedges; these fashions from France, it was said, were symbols of the Resistance. It was late on Sunday morning. She had been for a seemly walk along the pathways of Kensington Gardens with Greggie.

Selina took off her hat and laid it on the sofa beside her. She said, 'I've got a guest for lunch, Felix.' Felix was Colonel G. Felix Dobell who was head of a branch of the American Intelligence Service which occupied the top floor of the hotel next door to the club. He had been among a number of men invited to one of the club's dances, and there had selected Selina for himself.

Jane said, 'I'm having Nicholas Farringdon for lunch.'

'But he was here during the week.'

'Well, he's coming again. I went to a party with him.'

'Good,' said Selina. 'I like him.'

Jane said, 'Nicholas works with the American Intelligence. He probably knows your Colonel.'

It was found that the men had not met. They shared a table for four with the two girls, who waited on them, fetching the food from the hatch. Sunday lunch was the best meal of the week. Whenever one of the girls rose to fetch and carry, Felix Dobell half-rose in his chair, then sat down again, for courtesy. Nicholas lolled like an

Englishman possessed of *droits de seigneur* while the two girls served him.

The warden, a tall grey-skinned woman habitually dressed in grey, made a brief announcement that 'the Conservative M.P. was coming to give a pre-election discussion' on the following Tuesday.

Nicholas smiled widely so that his long dark face became even more good-looking. He seemed to like the idea of *giving* a discussion, and said so to the Colonel who amiably agreed with him. The Colonel seemed to be in love with the entire club, Selina being the centre and practical focus of his feelings in this respect. This was a common effect of the May of Teck Club on its male visitors, and Nicholas was enamoured of the entity in only one exceptional way, that it stirred his poetic sense to a point of exasperation, for at the same time he discerned with irony the process of his own thoughts, how he was imposing upon this society an image incomprehensible to itself.

The grey warden's conversational voice could be heard addressing grey-haired Greggie who sat with her at table, 'You see, Greggie, I can't be everywhere in the club at once.'

Jane said to her companions, 'That's the one fact that makes life bearable for us.'

'That is a very original idea,' said the American Colonel, but he was referring to something that Nicholas had said before Jane had spoken, when they were discussing the political outlook of the May of Teck Club. Nicholas had offered: 'They should be told not to vote at all, I mean persuaded not to vote at all. We could do without the government. We could manage with the monarchy, the House of Lords, the . . .'

Jane looked bored, as she had several times read this bit in the manuscript, and she rather wanted to discuss personalities, which always provided her with more real pleasure than any impersonal talk however light and fantastic, although she did not yet admit this fact in her aspiring brain. It was not till Jane had reached the apex of her career as a reporter and interviewer for the largest of women's journals that she found her right role in life, while still incorrectly subscribing to a belief that she was capable of thought – indeed, was demonstrating a capacity for it. But now she sat at table with Nicholas and longed for him to stop talking to the Colonel about the happy possibilities inherent in the delivery of political speeches to the May of Teck girls, and the different ways in which they might be corrupted. Jane felt guilty about her boredom. Selina laughed with poise when Nicholas said, next, 'We could do without a central government. It's bad for us, and what's worse, it's bad for the politicians . . .' but that he was as serious about this as it was possible for his self-mocking mind to be about anything, seemed to be apparent to the Colonel, who amazingly assured Nicholas, 'My wife Gareth also is a member of the Guild of Ethical Guardians in our town. She's a hard worker.'

Nicholas, reminding himself that poise was perfect balance, accepted this statement as a rational response. 'Who are the Ethical Guardians?' said Nicholas.

'They stand for the ideal of purity in the home. They keep a special guard on reading material. Many homes in our town will not accept literature unstamped by the Guardians' crest of honour.'

Nicholas now saw that the Colonel had understood him to hold ideals, and had connected them with the ideals of his wife Gareth, these being the only other ideals he could immediately lay hands on. It was the only explanation. Jane wanted to put everything straight. She said, 'Nicholas is an anarchist.'

'Ah no, Jane,' said the Colonel. 'That's being a bit hard on your author-friend.'

Selina had already begun to realise that Nicholas held unorthodox views about things to the point where they might be regarded as crackpot to the sort of people she was used to. She felt his unusualness was a weakness, and this weakness in an attractive man held desirability for her. There were two other men of her acquaintance who were vulnerable in some way. She was not perversely interested in this fact, so far as she felt no urge to hurt them; if she did so, it was by accident. What she liked about these men was that neither of them wished to possess her entirely. She slept with them happily because of this. She had another man-friend, a businessman of thirty-five, still in the Army, very wealthy, not weak. He was altogether possessive; Selina thought she might marry him eventually. In the meantime she looked at Nicholas as he conversed in this mad sequence with the Colonel, and thought she could use him.

They sat in the drawing-room and planned the afternoon which had developed into a prospective outing for four in the Colonel's car. By this time he had demanded to be called Felix.

He was about thirty-two. He was one of Selina's weak men. His weakness was an overwhelming fear of his wife, so that he took great pains not to be taken unawares in bed with Selina on their country weekends, even although his wife was in California. As he locked the door of the bedroom Felix would say, very worried, 'I wouldn't like to hurt Gareth,' or some such thing. The first time he did this Selina looked through the bathroom door, tall and beautiful with wide eyes, she looked at Felix to see what was the matter with him. He was still anxious and tried the door again. On the late Sunday mornings, when the bed was already uncomfortable with breakfast crumbs, he would sometimes fall into a muse and be far away. He might then say, 'I hope there's no way Gareth could come by knowledge of this hideout.' And so he was one of those who did not want to possess Selina entirely; and being beautiful and liable to provoke possessiveness, she found this all right provided the man was attractive to sleep with and be out with, and was a good dancer. Felix was blond with an appearance of reserved nobility which he must have inherited. He seldom said anything very humorous, but was willing to be gay. On this Sunday afternoon in the May of Teck Club he proposed to drive to Richmond, which was a long way by car from Knightsbridge in those days when petrol was so scarce that nobody went driving for pleasure except in an American's car, in the vague mistaken notion that their vehicles were supplied by 'American' oil, and so were not subject to the conscience of British austerity or the reproachful question about the necessity of the journey displayed at all places of public transport.

Jane, observing Selina's long glance of perfect balance and equanimity resting upon Nicholas, immediately foresaw that she would be disposed in the front seat with Felix while Selina stepped, with her arch-footed poise, into the back, where Nicholas would join her; and she foresaw that this arrangement would come about with effortless elegance. She had no objection to Felix, but she could not hope to win him for herself, having nothing to offer a man like Felix. She felt she had a certain something, though small, to offer Nicholas, this being her literary and brain-work side which Selina lacked. It was in fact a misunderstanding of Nicholas – she vaguely thought of him as a more attractive Rudi Bittesch – to imagine he would receive more pleasure and reassurance from a literary girl than simply a girl. It was the girl in Jane that had moved him to kiss her at the party;

she might have gone further with Nicholas without her literary leanings. This was a mistake she continued to make in her relations with men, inferring from her own preference for men of books and literature their preference for women of the same business. And it never really occurred to her that literary men, if they like women at all, do not want literary women but girls.

But Jane was presently proved right in her prediction about the seating arrangements in the car; and it was her repeated accuracy of intuition in such particulars as these which gave her confidence in her later career as a prophetic gossip-columnist.

Meantime the brown-lined drawing-room began to chirp into life as the girls came in from the dining-room bearing trays of coffee cups. The three spinsters, Greggie, Collie, and Jarvie, were introduced to the guests, as was their accustomed right. They sat in hard chairs and poured coffee for the young loungers. Collie and Jarvie were known to be in the process of a religious quarrel, but they made an effort to conceal their differences for the occasion. Jarvie, however, was agitated by the fact that her coffee cup had been filled too full by Collie. She laid the cup and swimming saucer on a table a little way behind her, and ignored it significantly. She was dressed to go out, with gloves, bag, and hat. She was presently going to take her Sunday-school class. The gloves were made of a stout green-brown suède. Jarvie smoothed them out on her lap, then fluttered her fingers over the cuffs, turning them back. They revealed the utility stamp, two half-moons facing the same way, which was the mark of price-controlled clothes and which, on dresses, where the mark was merely stamped on a tape sewn on the inside, everyone removed. Jarvie surveyed her gloves' irremovable utility mark with her head at a slight angle, as if considering some question connected with it. She then smoothed out the gloves again and jerkily adjusted her spectacles. Jane felt in a great panic to get married. Nicholas, on hearing that Jarvie was about to go to teach a Sunday-school class, was solicitous to inquire about it.

'I think we had better drop the subject of religion,' Jarvie said, as if in conclusion of an argument long in progress. Collie said, 'I thought we *had* dropped it. What a lovely day for Richmond!'

Selina slouched elegantly in her chair, untouched by the threat of becoming a spinster, as she would never be that sort of spinster, anyway. Jane recalled the beginning of the religious quarrel overheard on all floors, since it had taken place in the echoing wash-room on the second landing. Collie had at first accused Jarvie of failing to clean the sink after using it to wash up her dishes of stuff, which she surreptitiously cooked on her gas-ring where only kettles were lawfully permitted. Then, ashamed of her outburst, Collie had more loudly accused Jarvie of putting spiritual obstacles in her path 'just when you know I'm growing in grace'. Jarvie had then said something scornful about the Baptists as opposed to the true spirit of the Gospels. This religious row, with elaborations, had now lasted more than two weeks but the women were doing their best to conceal it. Collie now said to Jarvie, 'Are you going to waste your coffee with the milk in it?' This was a moral rebuke, for milk was on the ration. Jarvie turned, smoothed, patted and pulled straight the gloves on her lap and breathed in and out. Jane wanted to tear off her clothes and run naked into the street, screaming. Collie looked with disapproval at Jane's bare fat knees.

Greggie, who had very little patience with the two other elder members, had been winning her way with Felix, and had inquired what went on 'up there, next door', meaning

61

in the hotel, the top floor of which the American Intelligence was using, the lower floors being strangely empty and forgotten by the requisitioners.

'Ah, you'd be surprised, ma'am,' Felix said.

Greggie said she must show the men round the garden before they set off for Richmond. The fact that Greggie did practically all the gardening detracted from its comfort for the rest of the girls. Only the youngest and happiest girls could feel justified in using it to sit about in, as it was so much Greggie's toiled-at garden. Only the youngest and happiest could walk on the grass with comfort; they were not greatly given to scruples and consideration for others, by virtue of their unblighted spirits.

Nicholas had noticed a handsome bright-cheeked fair-haired girl standing, drinking down her coffee fairly quickly. She left the room with graceful speed when she had drunk her coffee.

Jane said, 'That's Joanna Childe who does elocution.'

Later, in the garden, while Greggie was conducting her tour, they heard Joanna's voice. Greggie was displaying her various particular items, rare plants reared from stolen cuttings, these being the only objects that Greggie would ever think of stealing. She boasted, like a true gardening woman, of her thefts and methods of acquiring snips of other people's rare plants. The sound of Joanna's afternoon pupil lilted down from her room.

Nicholas said, 'The voice is coming from up there, now. Last time, it came from the ground floor.'

'She uses her own room at weekends when the recreation room is used a lot. We're very proud of Joanna.'

Joanna's voice followed her pupil's.

Greggie said, 'This hollow shouldn't be there. It's where the bomb dropped. It just missed the house.'

'Were you in the house at the time?' said Felix.

'I was,' said Greggie. 'I was in bed. Next moment I was on the floor. All the windows were broken. And it's my suspicion there was a second bomb that didn't go off. I'm almost sure I saw it drop as I picked myself up off the floor. But the disposal squad found only the one bomb and removed it. Anyway, if there's a second it must have died a natural death by now. I'm talking about the year nineteen forty-two.'

Felix said, with his curious irrelevancy, 'My wife Gareth talks of coming over here with U.N.R.R.A. I wonder if she could put up at your club in transit for a week or two? I have to be back and forth, myself. She would be lonely in London.'

'It would have been lying underneath the hydrangeas on the right if I was correct,' Greggie said.

> The sea of faith
> Was once, too, at the full, and round earth's shore
> Lay like the folds of a bright girdle furled.
> But now I only hear
> Its melancholy, long, withdrawing roar,
> Retreating, to the breath
> Of the night-wind, down the vast edges drear
> And naked shingles of the world.

'We'd better be on our way to Richmond,' Felix said.

'We're awfully proud of Joanna,' said Greggie.

'A fine reader.'

'No, she recites from memory. But her pupils read, of course. It's elocution.'

Selina gracefully knocked some garden mud off her wedge shoes on the stone step, and the party moved inside.

The girls went to get ready. The men disappeared in the dark little downstairs cloakroom.

'That is a fine poem,' said Felix, for Joanna's voices were here, too, and the lesson had moved to *Kubla Khan*.

Nicholas almost said, 'She is orgiastical in her feeling for poetry. I can hear it in her voice,' but refrained in case the Colonel should say 'Really?' and he should go on to say, 'Poetry takes the place of sex for her, I think.'

'Really? She looked sexually fine to me.'

Which conversation did not take place, and Nicholas kept it for his notebooks.

They waited in the hall till the girls came down, Nicholas read the notice-board, advertising second-hand clothes for sale, or in exchange for clothing coupons. Felix stood back, a refrainer from such intrusions on the girls' private business, but tolerant of the other man's curiosity. He said, 'Here they come.'

The number and variety of muted noises-off were considerable. Laughter went on behind the folded doors of the first-floor dormitory. Someone was shovelling coal in the cellar, having left open the green baize door which led to those quarters. The telephone desk within the office rang distantly shrill with boy-friends, and various corresponding buzzes on the landings summoned the girls to talk. The sun broke through as the forecast had promised.

> Weave a circle round him thrice,
> And close your eyes with holy dread,
> For he on honey-dew hath fed,
> And drunk the milk of Paradise.

6

'Dear Dylan Thomas,' wrote Jane.

Downstairs, Nancy Riddle, who had finished her elocution lesson, was attempting to discuss with Joanna Childe the common eventualities arising from being a clergyman's daughter.

'My father's always in a filthy temper on Sundays. Is yours?'

'No, he's rather too occupied.'

'Father goes on about the Prayer Book. I must say, I agree with him there. It's out of date.'

'Oh, I think the Prayer Book's wonderful,' said Joanna. She had the Book of Common Prayer practically by heart, including the Psalms – especially the Psalms – which her father repeated daily at Matins and Evensong in the frequently empty church. In former years at the rectory Joanna had attended these services every day, and had made the responses from her pew, as it might be on 'Day 13', when her father would stand in his lofty meekness, robed in white over black, to read:

Let God arise, and let his enemies be scattered:

whereupon without waiting for pause Joanna would respond:

let them also that hate him flee before him.

The father continued:

Like as the smoke vanisheth, so shalt thou drive them away:

And Joanna came in swiftly:

and like as wax melteth at the fire, so let the ungodly perish
at the presence of God.

And so on had circled the Psalms, from Day 1 to Day 31
of the months, morning and evening, in peace and war; and
often the first curate, and then the second curate, took over
the office, uttering as it seemed to the empty pews, but by
faith to the congregations of the angels, the Englishly
rendered intentions of the sweet singer of Israel.

Joanna lit the gas-ring in her room in the May of Teck
Club and put on the kettle. She said to Nancy Riddle: 'The
Prayer Book is wonderful. There was a new version got up
in nineteen twenty-eight, but Parliament put it out. Just as
well, as it happened.'

'What's the Prayer Book got to do with them?'

'It's within their jurisdiction funnily enough.'

'I believe in divorce,' Nancy said.

'What's that got to do with the Prayer Book?'

'Well, it's all connected with the C. of E. and all the
arguing.'

Joanna mixed some powdered milk carefully with water
from the tap and poured the mixture upon two cups of tea.
She passed a cup to Nancy and offered saccharine tablets
from a small tin box. Nancy took one tablet, dropped it in
her tea, and stirred it. She had recently got involved with
a married man who talked of leaving his wife.

Joanna said, 'My father had to buy a new cloak to wear

over his cassock at funerals, he always catches cold at funerals. That means no spare coupons for me this year.'

Nancy said, 'Does he wear a cloak? He must be High. My father wears an overcoat; he's Low to Middle, of course.'

All through the first three weeks of July Nicholas wooed Selina and at the same time cultivated Jane and others of the May of Teck Club.

The sounds and sights impinging on him from the hall of the club intensified themselves, whenever he called, into one sensation, as if with a will of their own. He thought of the lines:

> Let us roll all our strength, and all
> Our sweetness up into one ball;

And I would like, he thought, to teach Joanna that poem or rather demonstrate it; and he made spasmodic notes of all this on the back pages of his *Sabbath* manuscript.

Jane told him everything that went on in the club. 'Tell me more,' he said. She told him things, in her clever way of intuition, which fitted his ideal of the place. In fact, it was not an unjust notion, that it was a miniature expression of a free society, that it was a community held together by the graceful attributes of a common poverty. He observed that at no point did poverty arrest the vitality of its members but rather nourished it. Poverty differs vastly from want, he thought.

'Hallo, Pauline?'
  'Yes?'
  'It's Jane.'
  'Yes?'

'I've got something to tell you. What's the matter?'

'I was resting.'

'Sleeping?'

'No, resting. I've just got back from the psychiatrist, he makes me rest after every session. I've got to lie down.'

'I thought you were finished with the psychiatrist. Are you not very well again?'

'This is a new one. Mummy found him, he's marvellous.'

'Well, I just wanted to tell you something, can you listen? Do you remember Nicholas Farringdon?'

'No, I don't think so. Who's he?'

'Nicholas . . . remember that last time on the roof at the May of Teck . . . Haiti, in a hut . . . among some palms, it was market day, everyone had gone to the market centre. Are you listening?'

We are in the summer of 1945 when he was not only enamoured of the May of Teck Club as an aesthetic and ethical conception of it, lovely frozen image that it was, but he presently slept with Selina on the roof.

> The mountains look on Marathon
>   And Marathon looks on the sea;
> And musing there an hour alone,
>   I dream'd that Greece might still be free;
> For standing on the Persians' grave,
> I could not deem myself a slave.

Joanna needs to know more life, thought Nicholas, as he loitered in the hall on one specific evening, but if she knew life she would not be proclaiming these words so sexually and matriarchally as if in the ecstatic act of suckling a divine child.

> At the top of the house the apples are laid in rows.

She continued to recite as he loitered in the hall. No one was about. Everyone was gathered somewhere else, in the drawing-room or in the bedrooms, sitting round wireless sets, tuning in to some special programme. Then one wireless, and another, roared forth louder by far than usual from the upper floors; others tuned in to the chorus, justified in the din by the voice of Winston Churchill. Joanna ceased. The wirelesses spoke forth their simultaneous Sinaitic predictions of what fate would befall the freedom-loving electorate should it vote for Labour in the forthcoming elections. The wirelesses suddenly started to reason humbly:

> We shall have Civil Servants . . .

The wirelesses changed their tones, they roared:

> No longer civil . . .

Then they were sad and slow:

> No longer . . .
> . . . *servants.*

Nicholas imagined Joanna standing by her bed, put out of business as it were, but listening, drawing it into her blood-stream. As in a dream of his own that depicted a dream of hers, he thought of Joanna in this immovable attitude, given up to the cadences of the wireless as if it did not matter what was producing them, the politician or herself. She was a proclaiming statue in his mind.

A girl in a long evening dress slid in the doorway, furtively. Her hair fell round her shoulders in a brown curl. Through the bemused mind of the loitering, listening man went the fact of a girl slipping furtively into the hall; she had a meaning, even if she had no meaningful intention.

She was Pauline Fox. She was returning from a taxi-ride round the park at the price of eight shillings. She had got into the taxi and told the driver to drive round, round anywhere, just drive. On such occasions the taxi-drivers suspected at first that she was driving out to pick up a man, then as the taxi circled the park and threepences ticked up on the meter, the drivers suspected she was mad, or even, perhaps, one of those foreign royalties still exiled in London: and they concluded one or the other when she ordered them back to the door to which she had summoned them by carefully pre-arranged booking. It was dinner with Jack Buchanan which Pauline held as an immovable idea to be established as fact at the May of Teck Club. In the day-time she worked in an office and was normal. It was dinner with Jack Buchanan that prevented her from dining with any other man, and caused her to wait in the hall for half an hour after the other members had gone to the dining-room, and to return surreptitiously half an hour later when nobody, or few, were about.

At times, when Pauline had been seen returning within so short a time, she behaved quite convincingly.

'Goodness, back already, Pauline! I thought you'd gone out to dinner with –'

'Oh! Don't talk to me. We've had a row.' Pauline, with one hand holding a handkerchief to her eye, and the other lifting the hem of her dress, would run sobbing up the stairs to her room.

'She must have had a row with Jack Buchanan again.

Funny she never brings Jack Buchanan here.'

'Do you believe it?'

'What?'

'That she goes out with Jack Buchanan?'

'Well, I've wondered.'

Pauline looked furtive, and Nicholas cheerfully said to her, 'Where have *you* been?'

She came and gazed into his face and said, 'I've been to dinner with Jack Buchanan.'

'You've missed Churchill's speech.'

'I know.'

'Did Jack Buchanan get rid of you the moment you had finished your dinner?'

'Yes. He did. We had a row.'

She shook back her shining hair. For this evening, she had managed to borrow the Schiaparelli dress. It was made of taffeta, with small side panniers stuck out with cleverly curved pads over the hips. It was coloured dark blue, green, orange and white in a floral pattern as from the Pacific Islands.

He said, 'I don't think I've ever seen such a gorgeous dress.'

'Schiaparelli,' she said.

He said, 'Is it the one you swap amongst yourselves?'

'Who told you that?'

'You look beautiful,' he replied.

She picked up the rustling skirt and floated away up the staircase.

Oh, girls of slender means!

The election speech having come to an end, everybody's wireless was turned off for a space, as if in reverence to what had just passed through the air.

He approached the office door which stood open. The

office was still empty. The warden came up behind him, having deserted her post for the duration of the speech.

'I'm still waiting for Miss Redwood.'

'I'll ring her again. No doubt she's been listening to the speech.'

Selina came down presently. Poise is perfect balance, an equanimity of body and mind. Down the staircase she floated, as it were even more realistically than had the sad communer with the spirit of Jack Buchanan a few moments ago floated up it. It might have been the same girl, floating upwards in a Schiaparelli rustle of silk with a shining hood of hair, and floating downwards in a slim skirt with a white-spotted blue blouse, her hair now piled high. The normal noises of the house began to throb again. 'Good evening,' said Nicholas.

> And all my days are trances,
>   And all my nightly dreams
> Are where thy dark eye glances,
>   And where thy footstep gleams –
> In what ethereal dances,
>   By what eternal streams!

'Now repeat,' said Joanna's voice.

'Come on then,' said Selina, stepping ahead of him into the evening light like a racer into the paddock, with a high disregard of all surrounding noises.

7

'Have you got a shilling for the meter?' said Jane.

'Poise is perfect balance, an equanimity of body and mind, complete composure whatever the social scene. Elegant dress, immaculate grooming, and perfect deportment all contribute to the attainment of self-confidence.'

'Have you got a shilling for two sixpences?'

'No. Anne's got a key that opens the meters, though.'

'Anne, are you in? What about a loan of the key?'

'If we all start using it too often we'll be found out.'

'Only this once. I've got brain-work to do.'

Now sleeps the crimson petal, now the white;

Selina sat, not yet dressed, on the edge of Nicholas's bed. She had a way of glancing sideways beneath her lashes that gave her command of a situation which might otherwise place her in a weakness.

She said, 'How can you bear to live here?'

He said, 'It does till one finds a flat.'

In fact he was quite content with his austere bed-sitting room. With the reckless ambition of a visionary, he pushed his passion for Selina into a desire that she, too, should accept and exploit the outlines of poverty in her life. He loved her as he loved his native country. He wanted Selina to be an ideal society personified amongst her bones, he wanted her beautiful limbs to obey her mind and heart like intelligent men and women, and for these to possess the same grace and beauty as her body. Whereas Selina's desires were comparatively humble, she only wanted, at that particular moment, a packet of hair-grips which had just then disappeared from the shops for a few weeks.

It was not the first instance of a man taking a girl to bed with the aim of converting her soul, but he, in great exasperation, felt that it was, and poignantly, in bed, willed and willed the awakening of her social conscience. After which, he sighed softly into his pillow with a limp sense of achievement, and presently rose to find, with more exasperation than ever, that he had not in the least conveyed his vision of perfection to the girl. She sat on the bed and glanced around beneath her lashes. He was experienced in girls sitting on his bed, but not in girls as cool as Selina about their beauty, and such beauty as hers. It was incredible to him that she should not share with him an understanding of the lovely attributes of dispossession and poverty, her body was so austere and economically furnished.

She said, 'I don't know how you can live in this place, it's like a cell. Do you cook on that thing?' She meant the gas grill.

He said, while it dawned upon him that his love affair with Selina remained a love affair on his side only, 'Yes, of course. Would you like some bacon and egg?'

'Yes,' she said, and started to dress.

He took hope again, and brought out his rations. She was accustomed to men who got food from the black market.

'After the twenty-second of this month,' said Nicholas, 'we are to get two and a half ounces of tea – two ounces one week and three ounces the next.'

'How much do we get now?'

'Two ounces every week. Two ounces of butter; margarine, four ounces.'

She was amused. She laughed for a long time. She said, 'You sound so funny.'

'Christ, so I do!' he said.

'Have you used all your clothing coupons?'

'No, I've got thirty-four left.'

He turned the bacon in the pan. Then, on a sudden thought, he said, 'Would you like some clothing coupons?'

'Oh yes, please.'

He gave her twenty, ate some bacon with her, and took her home in a taxi.

He said, 'I've arranged about the roof.'

She said, 'Well, see and arrange about the weather.'

'We can go to the pictures if it's raining,' he said.

He had arranged to have access to the roof through the top floor of the hotel next door, occupied as it was by American Intelligence, which organisation he served in another part of London. Colonel Dobell, who, up to ten days ago, would have opposed this move, now energetically supported it. The reason for this was that his wife Gareth was preparing to join him in London and he was anxious to situate Selina in another context, as he put it.

In the north of California, up a long drive, Mrs G. Felix Dobell had not only resided, but held meetings of the Guardians of Ethics. Now she was coming to London, for she said that a sixth sense told her Felix was in need of her presence there.

Now sleeps the crimson petal, now the white;

Nicholas greatly desired to make love to Selina on the roof, if needs must be on the roof. He arranged everything as precisely as a practised incendiary.

The flat roof of the club, accessible only by the slit window on the top floor, was joined to a similar flat roof of the neighbouring hotel by a small gutter. The hotel had been requisitioned and its rooms converted into offices for the use of the American Intelligence. Like many other requisitioned premises in London, it had been overcrowded with personnel during the war in Europe, and now was practically unoccupied. Only the top floor of this hotel, where uniformed men worked mysteriously day and night, and the ground floor, which was guarded day and night by two American servicemen, and served by night- and day-porters who worked the lift, were in use. Nobody could enter this house without a pass. Nicholas obtained a pass quite easily, and he also by means of a few words and a glance obtained the ambivalent permission of Colonel Dobell, whose wife was already on her journey, to move into a large attic office which was being used as a typing pool. Nicholas was given a courtesy desk there. This attic had a hatch door leading to the flat roof.

The weeks had passed, and since in the May of Teck Club they were weeks of youth in the ethos of war, they were capable of accommodating quick happenings and reversals, rapid formations of intimate friendships, and a range of lost and discovered loves that in later life and in peace would take years to happen, grow, and fade. The May of Teck girls were nothing if not economical. Nicholas, who was past his youth, was shocked at heart by their week-by-week emotions.

'I thought you said she was in love with the boy.'

'So she was.'

'Well, wasn't it only last week he died? You said he died of dysentery in Burma.'

'Yes I know. But she met this naval type on Monday, she's madly in love with him.'

76

'She can't be in love with him,' said Nicholas.

'Well, they've got a lot in common she says.'

'A lot in common? It's only Wednesday now.'

> Like one, that on a lonesome road
> Doth walk in fear and dread,
> And having once turned round, walks on,
> And turns no more his head;
> Because he knows a frightful fiend
> Doth close behind him tread.

'Joanna's marvellous at that one, I love it.'

'Poor Joanna.'

'Why do you say poor Joanna?'

'Well, she never gets any fun, no men-friends.'

'She's terribly attractive.'

'Frightfully attractive. Why doesn't someone do something about Joanna?'

Jane said, 'Look here, Nicholas, there's something you ought to know about Huy Throvis-Mew as a firm and George himself as a publisher.'

They were sitting in the offices of Throvis-Mew, high above Red Lion Square; but George was out.

'He's a crook,' said Nicholas.

'Well, that would be putting it a bit strongly,' she said.

'He's a crook with subtleties.'

'It's not quite that, either. It's a psychological thing about George. He's got to get the better of an author.'

'I know that,' Nicholas said. 'I had a long emotional letter from him making a lot of complaints about my book.'

'He wants to break down your confidence, you see, and then present you with a rotten contract to sign. He finds out the author's weak spot. He always attacks the bit the author likes best. He –'

'I know that,' said Nicholas.

'I'm only telling you because I like you,' Jane said. 'In fact, it's part of my job to find out the author's weak spot, and report to George. But I like you, and I'm telling you all this because –'

'You and George,' said Nicholas, 'draw me a tiny bit closer to understanding the Sphinx's inscrutable smile. And I'll tell you another fact.'

Beyond the grimy window rain fell from a darkening sky on the bomb-sites of Red Lion Square. Jane had looked out in an abstract pose before making her revelation to Nicholas. She now actually noticed the scene, it made her eyes feel miserable and her whole life appeared steeped in equivalent misery. She was disappointed in life, once more.

'I'll tell you another fact,' said Nicholas. 'I'm a crook too. What are you crying for?'

'I'm crying for myself,' said Jane. 'I'm going to look for another job.'

'Will you write a letter for me?'

'What sort of a letter?'

'A crook-letter. From Charles Morgan to myself. Dear Mr Farringdon, When first I received your manuscript I was tempted to place it aside for my secretary to return to you with some polite excuse. But as happy chance would have it, before passing your work to my secretary, I flicked over the pages and my eyes lit on . . .'

'Lit on what?' said Jane.

'I'll leave that to you. Only choose one of the most concise and brilliant passages when you come to write the letter. That will be difficult, I admit, since all are equally brilliant. But choose the piece you like best. Charles Morgan is to say he read that one piece, and then the whole, avidly, from start to finish. He is to say it's a work of genius. He congratulates me on a work of genius, you realise. Then I show the letter to George.'

Jane's life began to sprout once more, green with possibility. She recalled that she was only twenty-three, and smiled.

'Then I show the letter to George,' Nicholas said, 'and I tell him he can keep his contract and –'

George arrived. He looked busily at them both. Simultaneously, he took off his hat, looked at his watch, and said to Jane, 'What's the news?'

Nicholas said, 'Ribbentrop is captured.'

George sighed.

'No news,' said Jane. 'Nobody's rung at all. No letters, nobody's been, nobody's rung us up. Don't worry.'

George went into his inner office. He came out again immediately.

'Did you get my letter?' he said to Nicholas.

'No,' said Nicholas, 'which letter?'

'I wrote, let me see, the day before yesterday, I think. I wrote –'

'Oh, that letter,' said Nicholas. 'Yes, I believe I did receive a letter.'

George went away into his inner office.

Nicholas said to Jane, in a good, loud voice, that he was going for a stroll in the park now that the rain had stopped, and that it was lovely having nothing to do but dream beautiful dreams all the day long.

'Yours very sincerely and admiringly, Charles Morgan,' wrote Jane. She opened the door of her room and shouted, 'Turn down the wireless a bit, I've got to do some brainwork before supper.'

On the whole, they were proud of Jane's brain-work and her connection with the world of books. They turned down all the wirelesses on the landing.

She read over the first draft of the letter, then very carefully began again, making an authentic-looking letter in a small but mature hand such as Charles Morgan might use. She had no idea what Charles Morgan's handwriting looked like; and had no reason to find out, since George would certainly not know either, and was not to be allowed to retain the document. She had an address at Holland Park which Nicholas had supplied. She wrote this at the top of her writing paper, hoping that it looked all right, and assuring herself that it did since many nice people did not attempt to have their letter-heads printed in war-time and thus make unnecessary demands on the nation's labour.

She had finished by the time the supper-bell rang. She folded the letter with meticulous neatness, having before her eyes the pencil-line features of Charles Morgan's photograph. Jane calculated that this letter by Charles Morgan which she had just written was worth at least fifty pounds to Nicholas. George would be in a terrible state of conflict when he saw it. Poor Tilly, George's wife, had told her that when George was persecuted by an author, he went on and on about it for hours.

Nicholas was coming to the club after supper to spend the evening, having at last persuaded Joanna to give a special recital of *The Wreck of the Deutschland*. It was to be recorded on a tape-machine that Nicholas had borrowed from the news-room of a Government office.

Jane joined the throng in its descent to supper. Only Selina loitered above, finishing off her evening's disciplinary recitation:

... Elegant dress, immaculate grooming, and perfect deportment all contribute to the attainment of self-confidence.

The warden's car stopped piercingly outside as the girls
reached the lower floor. The warden drove a car as she would
have driven a man had she possessed one. She strode, grey,
into her office and shortly afterwards joined them in the
dining-room, banging on the water-jug with her fork for
silence, as she always did when about to make an announcement. She announced that an American visitor, Mrs G. Felix
Dobell, would address the club on Friday evening on the
subject, 'Western Woman: Her Mission'. Mrs Dobell was a
leading member of the Guardians of Ethics and had recently
come to join her husband who was serving with the United
States Intelligence Service stationed in London.

After supper Jane was struck by a sense of her treachery
to the establishment of Throvis-Mew, and to George with
whom she was paid to conspire in the way of business. She
was fond of old George, and began to reflect on his kindly
qualities. Without the slightest intention of withdrawing
from her conspiracy with Nicholas, she gazed at the letter
she had written and wondered what to do about her feelings.
She decided to telephone to his wife, Tilly, and have a
friendly chat about something.

Tilly was delighted. She was a tiny redhead of lively
intelligence and small information, whom George kept well
apart from the world of books, being experienced in wives.
To Tilly, this was a great deprivation, and she loved nothing
better than to keep in touch, through Jane, with the book
business and to hear Jane say, 'Well, Tilly, it's a question of
one's raison d'être.' George tolerated this friendship, feeling
that it established himself with Jane. He relied on Jane. She
understood his ways.

Jane was usually bored by Tilly, who, although she had not exactly been a cabaret dancer, imposed on the world of books, whenever she was given the chance, a high leg-kicker's spirit which played on Jane's nerves, since she herself was newly awed by the gravity of literature in general. She felt Tilly was altogether too frivolous about the publishing and writing scene, and moreover failed to realise this fact. But her heart in its treachery now swelled with an access of warmth for Tilly. She telephoned and invited her to supper on Friday. Jane had already calculated that, if Tilly should be a complete bore, they would be able to fill in an hour with Mrs G. Felix Dobell's lecture. The club was fairly eager to see Mrs Dobell, having already seen a certain amount of her husband as Selina's escort, rumoured to be her lover. 'There's a talk on Friday by an American woman on the Western Woman's Mission, but we won't listen to that, it would be a bore,' Jane said, contradicting her resolution in her effusive anxiety to sacrifice anything, anything to George's wife, now that she had betrayed and was about to deceive George.

Tilly said, 'I always love the May of Teck. It's like being back at school.' Tilly always said that, it was infuriating.

Nicholas arrived early with his tape-recorder, and sat in the recreation room with Joanna, waiting for the audience to drift in from supper. She looked to Nicholas very splendid and Nordic, as from a great saga.

'Have you lived here long?' said Nicholas sleepily, while he admired her big bones. He was sleepy because he had spent most of the previous night on the roof with Selina.

'About a year. I daresay I'll die here,' she said with the conventional contempt of all members for the club.

He said, 'You'll get married.'

'No, no.' She spoke soothingly, as to a child who had just been prevented from spooning jam into the stew.

A long shriek of corporate laughter came from the floor immediately above them. They looked at the ceiling and realised that the dormitory girls were as usual exchanging those R.A.F. anecdotes which needed an audience hilariously drunken, either with alcohol or extreme youth, to give them point.

Greggie had appeared, and cast her eyes up to the laughter as she came towards Joanna and Nicholas. She said, 'The sooner that dormitory crowd gets married and gets out of the club, the better. I've never known such a rowdy dormitory crowd in all my years in the club. Not a farthing's worth of intelligence between them.'

Collie arrived and sat down next to Nicholas. Greggie said, 'I was saying about the dormitory girls up there: they ought to get married and get out.'

This was also, in reality, Collie's view. But she always opposed Greggie on principle and, moreover, in company she felt that a contradiction made conversation. 'Why should they get married? Let them enjoy themselves while they're young.'

'They need marriage to enjoy themselves properly,' Nicholas said, 'for sexual reasons.'

Joanna blushed. Nicholas added, 'Heaps of sex. Every night for a month, then every other night for two months, then three times a week for a year. After that, once a week.' He was adjusting the tape-recorder, and his words were like air.

'If you're trying to shock us, young man, we're unshockable,' said Greggie, with a delighted glance round the four walls which were not accustomed to this type of talk, for, after all, it was the public recreation room.

'I'm shockable,' said Joanna. She was studying Nicholas with an apologetic look.

Collie did not know what attitude she should take up. Her fingers opened the clasp of her bag and snapped it shut again; then they played a silent tip-tap on its worn bulging leather sides. Then she said, 'He isn't trying to shock us. He's very realistic. If one is growing in grace – I would go so far as to say when one *has* grown in grace – one can take realism, sex and so forth in one's stride.'

Nicholas beamed lovingly at this.

Collie gave a little half-cough, half-laugh, much encouraged in the success of her frankness. She felt modern, and continued excitedly. 'It's a question of what you never have you never miss, of course.'

Greggie put on a puzzled air, as if she genuinely did not know what Collie was talking about. After thirty years' hostile fellowship with Collie, of course she did quite well understand that Collie had a habit of skipping several stages in the logical sequence of her thoughts, and would utter apparently disconnected statements, especially when confused by an unfamiliar subject or the presence of a man.

'Whatever do you mean?' said Greggie. '*What* is a question of what you never have you never miss?'

'Sex, of course,' Collie said, her voice unusually loud with the effort of the topic. 'We were discussing sex and getting married. I say, of course, there's a lot to be said for marriage, but if you never have it you never miss it.'

Joanna looked at the two excited women with meek compassion. To Nicholas she looked stronger than ever in her meekness, as she regarded Greggie and Collie at their rivalry to be uninhibited.

'What do you mean, Collie?' Greggie said. 'You're quite

wrong there, Collie. One does miss sex. The Body has a life of its own. We do miss what we haven't had, you and I. Biologically. Ask Sigmund Freud. It is revealed in dreams. The absent touch of the warm limbs at night, the absent –'

'Just a minute,' said Nicholas, holding up his hand for silence, in the pretence that he was tuning-in to his empty tape-machine. He could see that the two women would go to any lengths, now they had got started.

'Open the door, please.' From behind the door came the warden's voice and the rattle of the coffee tray. Before Nicholas could leap up to open it for her she had pushed into the room with some clever manoeuvring of hand and foot like a business-like parlourmaid.

'The Beatific Vision does not appear to *me* to be an adequate compensation for what we miss,' Greggie said conclusively, getting in a private thrust at Collie's religiosity.

While coffee was being served and the girls began to fill the room, Jane entered, fresh from her telephone conversation with Tilly, and, feeling somewhat absolved by it, she handed over to Nicholas her brain-work letter from Charles Morgan. While reading it, he was handed a cup of coffee. In the process of taking the cup he splashed some coffee on the letter.

'Oh, you've ruined it!' Jane said. 'I'll have to do it all over again.'

'It looks more authentic than ever,' Nicholas said. 'Naturally, if I've received a letter from Charles Morgan telling me I'm a genius, I am going to spend a lot of time reading it over and over, in the course of which the letter must begin to look a bit worn. Now, are you sure George will be impressed by Morgan's name?'

'Very,' said Jane.

'Do you mean you're very sure or that George will be very impressed?'

'I mean both.'

'It would put me off, if I were George.'

The recital of *The Wreck of the Deutschland* started presently. Joanna stood with her book ready.

'Not a hush from anybody,' said the warden, meaning, 'Not a sound.' – 'Not a hush,' she said, 'because this instrument of Mr Farringdon's apparently registers the drop of a pin.'

One of the dormitory girls, who sat mending a ladder in a stocking, carefully caused her needle to fall on the parquet floor, then bent and picked it up again. Another dormitory girl who had noticed the action snorted a suppressed laugh. Otherwise there was silence but for the quiet purr of the machine waiting for Joanna.

Thou mastering me
God! giver of breath and bread;
World's strand, sway of the sea;
Lord of living and dead;
Thou hast bound bones and veins in me, fastened me
flesh,
And after it almost unmade ...

8

A scream of panic from the top floor penetrated the house as Jane returned to the club on Friday afternoon, the 27th of July. She had left the office early to meet Tilly at the club. She did not feel that the scream of panic meant anything special. Jane climbed the last flight of stairs. There was another more piercing scream, accompanied by excited voices. Screams of panic in the club might relate to a laddered stocking or a side-splitting joke.

When she reached the top landing, she saw that the commotion came from the wash-room. There, Anne and Selina, with two of the dormitory girls, were attempting to extricate from the little slit window another girl who had evidently been attempting to climb out and had got stuck. She was struggling and kicking without success, exhorted by various instructions from the other girls. Against their earnest advice, she screamed aloud from time to time. She had taken off her clothes for the attempt and her body was covered with a greasy substance; Jane immediately hoped it had not been taken from her own supply of cold cream which stood in a jar on her dressing-table.

'Who is it?' Jane said, with a close inspective look at the girl's unidentifiable kicking legs and wriggling bottom which were her only visible portions.

Selina brought a towel which she attempted to fasten round the girl's waist with a safety-pin. Anne kept imploring the girl not to scream, and one of the others went to the top of the stairs to look over the banister in the hope that nobody in authority was being unduly attracted upward.

'Who is it?' Jane said.

Anne said, 'I'm afraid it's Tilly.'

'Tilly!'

'She was waiting downstairs and we brought her up here for a lark. She said it was like being back at school, here at the club, so Selina showed her the window. She's just half an inch too large, though. Can't you get her to shut up?'

Jane spoke softly to Tilly. 'Every time you scream,' she said, 'it makes you swell up more. Keep quiet, and we'll work you out with wet soap.'

Tilly went quiet. They worked on her for ten minutes, but she remained stuck by the hips. Tilly was weeping. 'Get George,' she said at last, 'get him on the phone.'

Nobody wanted to fetch George. He would have to come upstairs. Doctors were the only males who climbed the stairs, and even then they were accompanied by one of the staff.

Jane said, 'Well, I'll get somebody.' She was thinking of Nicholas. He had access to the roof from the Intelligence Headquarters; a hefty push from the roof-side of the window might be successful in releasing Tilly. Nicholas had intended to come to the club after supper to hear the lecture and observe, in a jealous complex of curiosity, the wife of Selina's former lover. Felix himself was to be present.

Jane decided to telephone and beg Nicholas to come immediately and help with Tilly. He could then have supper at the club, his second supper, Jane reflected, that week. He might now be home from work, he usually returned to his room at about six o'clock.

'What's the time?' said Jane.

Tilly was weeping, with a sound that threatened a further outburst of screams.

'Just on six,' said Anne.

Selina looked at her watch to see if this was so, then walked towards her room.

'Don't leave her, I'm getting help,' Jane said. Selina opened the door of her room, but Anne stood gripping Tilly's ankles. As Jane reached the next landing she heard Selina's voice.

'Poise is perfect balance, an equanimity . . .'

Jane laughed foolishly to herself and descended to the telephone boxes as the clock in the hall struck six o'clock.

It struck six o'clock on that evening of July 27th. Nicholas had just returned to his room. When he heard of Tilly's predicament he promised eagerly to go straight to the Intelligence Headquarters, and on to the roof.

'It's no joke,' Jane said.

'I'm not saying it's a joke.'

'You sound cheerful about it. Hurry up. Tilly's crying her eyes out.'

'As well she might, seeing Labour have got in.'

'Oh, hurry up. We'll all be in trouble if –'

He had rung off.

At that hour Greggie came in from the garden to hang about the hall, awaiting the arrival of Mrs Dobell who was to speak after supper. Greggie would take her into the warden's sitting-room, there to drink dry sherry till the supper-bell went. Greggie hoped also to induce Mrs Dobell to be escorted round the garden before supper.

A distant anguished scream descended the staircase.

'Really,' Greggie said to Jane, who was emerging from the telephone box, 'this club has gone right down. What are visitors to think? Who's screaming up there on the top floor? It sounds exactly as it must have been when this house was in private hands. You girls behave exactly like servant girls in the old days when the master and mistress were absent. Romping and yelling.'

> Make me thy lyre, even as the forest is:
> What if my leaves are falling like its own!
> The tumult of thy mighty harmonies.

'George, I want George,' Tilly wailed thinly from far above. Then someone on the top floor thoughtfully turned on the wireless to all-drowning pitch:

> There were angels dining at the Ritz
> And a nightingale sang in Berkeley Square.

And Tilly could be heard no more. Greggie looked out of the open front door and returned. She looked at her watch. 'Six-fifteen,' she said. 'She should be here at six-fifteen. Tell them to turn down the wireless up there. It looks so vulgar, so bad . . .'

'You mean it sounds so vulgar, so bad.' Jane was keeping an eye out for the taxi which she hoped would bring Nicholas, at any moment, to the functional hotel next door.

'Once again,' said Joanna's voice clearly from the third floor to her pupil. 'The last three stanzas again, please.'

> Drive my dead thoughts over the universe
> Like withered leaves to quicken a new birth!

Jane was suddenly overcome by a deep envy of Joanna, the source of which she could not locate exactly at that hour of her youth. The feeling was connected with an inner knowledge of Joanna's disinterestedness, her ability, a gift, to forget herself and her personality. Jane felt suddenly miserable, as one who has been cast out of Eden before realising that it had in fact been Eden. She recalled two ideas about Joanna that she had gathered from various observations made by Nicholas: that Joanna's enthusiasm for poetry was limited to one kind, and that Joanna was the slightest bit melancholy on the religious side; these thoughts failed to comfort Jane.

Nicholas arrived in a taxi and disappeared in the hotel entrance. As Jane started to run upstairs another taxi drew up. Greggie said, 'Here's Mrs Dobell. It's twenty-two minutes past six.'

Jane bumped into several of the girls who were spilling in lively groups out of the dormitories. She thrust her way through their midst, anxious to reach Tilly and tell her that help was near.

'Jane-*ee*!' said a girl. 'Don't be so bloody rude, you nearly pushed me over the banister to my death.'

But Jane was thumping upward.

Now sleeps the crimson petal, now the white;

Jane arrived at the top floor to find Anne and Selina frantically clothing Tilly's lower half to make her look decent. They had got as far as the stockings. Anne was holding a leg while Selina, long-fingered, smoothed the stocking over it.

'Nicholas has come. Is he out on the roof yet?'

Tilly moaned, 'Oh, I'm dying. I can't stand it any more. Fetch *George*, I want George.'

'Here's Nicholas,' said Selina, tall enough to see him emerging from the low doorway of the hotel attic, as he had lately done on the calm summer nights. He stumbled over a rug which had been bundled beside the door. It was one of the rugs they had brought out to lie on. He recovered his balance, started walking quickly over towards them, then fell flat on his face. A clock struck the half-hour. Jane heard herself say in a loud voice, 'It's half past six.' Suddenly, Tilly was sitting on the bathroom floor beside her. Anne, too, was on the floor crumpled with her arm over her eyes as if trying to hide her presence. Selina lay stunned against the door. She opened her mouth to scream, and probably did scream, but it was then that the rumbling began to assert itself from the garden below, mounting swiftly to a mighty crash. The house trembled again, and the girls who had tried to sit up were thrown flat. The floor was covered with bits of glass, and Jane's blood flowed from somewhere in a trickle, while some sort of time passed silently by. Sensations of voices, shouts, mounting footsteps and falling plaster brought the girls back to various degrees of responsiveness. Jane saw, in an unfocused way, the giant face of Nicholas peering through the open slit of the little window. He was exhorting them to get up quick.

'There's been an explosion in the garden.'

'Greggie's bomb,' Jane said, grinning at Tilly. 'Greggie was right,' she said. This was a hilarious statement, but Tilly did not laugh, she closed her eyes and lay back. Tilly was only half-dressed and looked very funny indeed. Jane then laughed loudly at Nicholas, but he too had no sense of humour.

Down in the street the main body of the club had congregated, having been in one of the public rooms on the ground floor at the time of the explosion, or else lingering in the dormitories. There, the explosion had been heard more than it was felt. Two ambulances had arrived and a third was approaching. Some of the more dazed among the people were being treated for shock in the hall of the neighbouring hotel.

Greggie was attempting to assure Mrs Felix Dobell that she had foreseen and forewarned the occurrence. Mrs Dobell, a handsome matron of noticeable height, stood out on the edge of the pavement, taking little notice of Greggie. She was looking at the building with a surveyor's eye, and was possessed of that calm which arises from a misunderstanding of the occasion's true nature, for although she was shaken by the explosion, Mrs Dobell assumed that belated bombs went off every day in Britain, and, content to find herself intact, and slightly pleased to have shared a war experience, was now curious as to what routine would be adopted in the emergency. She said, 'When do you calculate the dust will settle?'

Greggie said, yet once more, 'I knew that live bomb was in that garden. I knew it. I was always saying that bomb was there. The bomb-disposal squad missed it, they missed it.'

Some faces appeared at an upper bedroom. The window opened. A girl started to shout, but had to withdraw her head; she was choking with the dust that was still surrounding the house in clouds.

It was as difficult to discern the smoke, when it began to show, amongst the dust. A gas-main had, in fact, been ruptured by the explosion and a fire started to crawl along the basement from the furnaces. It started to crawl and then it flared. A roomful of flame suddenly roared in the ground-floor offices, lapping against the large window-panes, feeling for the woodwork, while Greggie continued to shrill at Mrs Dobell above the clamour of the girls, the street-crowd, the ambulances, and the fire-engines. 'It was ten chances to one we might have been in the garden when the bomb went off. I was going to take you round the garden before supper. We would have been buried, dead, killed. It was ten to one, Mrs Dobell.'

Mrs Dobell said, as one newly enlightened, 'This is a terrible incident.' And being more shaken than she appeared to be, she added, 'This is a time that calls for the exercise of discretion, the woman's prerogative.' This saying was part of the lecture she had intended to give after supper. She looked round in the crowd for her husband. The warden, whose more acute shock-effects had preceded Mrs Dobell's by a week, was being carried off through the crowd on a stretcher.

'Felix!' yelled Mrs Dobell. He was coming out of the hotel adjoining the club, with his olive-greenish khaki uniform dusky with soot and streaked as with black oil. He had been investigating the back premises of the club. He said: 'The brick-work of the walls looks unsteady. The top half of the fire-escape has collapsed. There are some girls trapped up there. The firemen are directing them up to the top floor; they'll have to be brought through the skylight on to the roof.'

'Who?' said Lady Julia.

'Jane Wright speaking. I rang you last week to see if you could find out some more about –'

'Oh yes. Well, I'm afraid there's very little information from the F.O. They never comment officially, you know. From what I can gather, the man was making a complete nuisance of himself, preaching against the local super-stitions. He had several warnings and apparently he got what he asked for. How did you come to know him?'

'He was friendly with some of the girls at the May of Teck Club when he was a civilian, I mean before he joined this Order. He was there on the night of the tragedy, in fact, and –'

'It probably turned his brain. Something must have affected his brain, anyhow, because from what I gather unofficially he was a complete . . .'

The skylight, although it had been bricked up by someone's hysterical order, at that time in the past when a man had penetrated the attic-floor of the club to visit a girl, was not beyond being unbricked by the firemen. It was all a question of time.

Time was not a large or present fact to those girls of the May of Teck Club, thirteen of them, who, with Tilly Throvis-Mew, remained in the upper storeys of the building when, following the explosion in the garden, fire broke out in the house. A large portion of the perfectly safe fire-escape which had featured in so many safety-instruction regulations, so many times read out to the members at so many supper-times, now lay in zigzag fragments among the earthy mounds and upturned roots of the garden.

Time, which was an immediate onward-rushing enemy to the onlookers in the street and the firemen on the roof, was only a small far-forgotten event to the girls; for they were stunned not only by the force of the explosion, but, when they recovered and looked round, still more by the sudden dislocation of all familiar appearances. A chunk of the back wall of the house gaped to the sky. There, in 1945, they were as far removed from the small fact of time as weightless occupants of a space-rocket. Jane got up, ran to her room, and with animal instinct snatched and gobbled a block of chocolate which remained on her table. The sweet stuff assisted her recovery. She turned to the wash-rooms where Tilly, Anne, and Selina were slowly rising to their feet. There were shouts from the direction of the roof. An unrecognised face looked in the slit window, and a large hand wrenched the loose frame away from it.

But the fire had already started to spread up the main staircase, preceded by heraldic puffs of smoke, the flames sidling up the banisters.

The girls who had been in their rooms on the second and third floors at the time of the explosion had been less shaken than those at the top of the house, since there some serious defect in the masonry had been caused indirectly by a bombardment early in the war. The girls on the second and third floors were cut and bruised, but were stunned by the sound of the blast rather than the house-shaking effects of it.

Some of the second-floor dormitory girls had been quick and alert enough to slip down the staircase and out into the street, in the interval between the explosion of the bomb and the start of the fire. The remaining ten, when they variously attempted to escape by that route, met the fire and retreated upward.

Joanna and Nancy Riddle, having finished their elocution lessons, had been standing at the door of Joanna's room when the bomb went off, and so had escaped the glass from the window. Joanna's hand was cut, however, by the glass from a tiny travelling clock which she had been winding at the time. It was Joanna who, when the members shrieked at the sight of the fire, gave the last shriek, then shouted: 'The fire-escape!' Pauline Fox fled behind her, and the others followed along the second-floor corridors and up the narrow back staircase to the third-floor passage-way where the fire-escape window had always stood. This was now a platform open to the summer evening sky, for here the wall had fallen away and the fire-escape with it. Plaster tumbled from the bricks as the ten women crowded to the spot that had once been the fire-escape landing. They were still looking in a bewildered way for the fire-escape stairway. Voices of firemen shouted at them from the garden. Voices came from the direction of the flat roof above, and then one voice clearly through a megaphone ordered them back, lest the piece of floor they stood on should collapse.

The voice said, 'Proceed to the top floor.'

'Jack will wonder what's happened to me,' said Pauline Fox. She was first up the back stairs to the wash-rooms where Anne, Selina, Jane, and Tilly were now on their feet, having steadied themselves on learning of the fire. Selina was taking off her skirt.

Above their heads, set in a sloping ceiling, was the large square outline of the old, bricked-in skylight. Men's voices, the scrabble of ladders and loud thumps of bricks being tested, came down from this large square. The men were evidently trying to find a means of opening the skylight to release the girls, who meanwhile stared up at the square mark in the ceiling. Tilly said, 'Won't it open?' Nobody answered, because the girls of the club knew the answer. Everyone in the club had heard the legend of the man who had got in by the skylight and, some said, been found in bed with a girl.

Now Selina stood on the lavatory seat and jumped up to the slit window. She slid through it to the roof with an easy diagonal movement. There were now thirteen women in the wash-room. They stood in the alert, silent attitude of jungle-danger, listening for further instruction from the megaphone on the roof outside.

Anne Baberton followed Selina through the slit window, with difficulty, because she was flustered. But a man's two hands came up to the window to receive her. Tilly Throvis-Mew began to sob. Pauline Fox ripped off her dress and then her underclothes until she was altogether naked. She had an undernourished body; there would have been no difficulty for her in getting through the slit window fully clothed, but she went naked as a fish.

Only Tilly sobbed heavily, but the rest of the girls were trembling. The noises from the sloping roof ceased as the firemen jumped down from investigating the skylight on to the flat roof area; footsteps beat and shuffled there, beyond the slit window, where throughout the summer Selina had lain with Nicholas, wrapped in rugs, under Orion's Belt and the Plough, which constituted the only view in Greater London that remained altogether intact.

Within the wash-room the eleven remaining women heard a fireman's voice addressing them through the window, against the simultaneous blare of megaphone instructions to the firemen. The man at the window said, 'Stay where you are. Don't panic. We're sending for tools to uncover the brickwork over the skylight. We won't be long. It's a question of time. We are doing everything we can to get you out. Remain where you are. Don't panic. It's just a question of time.'

The question of time opened now as a large thing in the lives of the eleven listeners.

Twenty-eight minutes had passed since the bomb had exploded in the garden. Felix Dobell joined Nicholas Farringdon on the flat roof after the fire started. They assisted the three slim girls through the window. Anne and naked Pauline Fox had been huddled into the two blankets of variable purpose, and hustled through the roof-hatch of the neighbouring hotel, the back windows of which had been smashed by the blast. Nicholas was as fleetingly impressed as was possible in the emergency, by the fact that Selina allowed the other girls to take the blankets. She lingered, shivering a little, but with an appealing grace, like a wounded roe deer, in her white petticoat and bare feet. Nicholas thought she was lingering for his sake, since Felix had disappeared with the two other girls to help them down to the first-aid ambulances. He left Selina standing thoughtfully on the hotel side of the roof, and returned to the slit window of the club to see for himself if any of the remaining girls were slim enough to escape by that way. It had been said by the firemen that the building might collapse within the next twenty minutes.

As he approached the slit window Selina slipped past him and, clutching the sill, heaved herself up again.

'Come down, what are you doing?' Nicholas said. He tried to grasp her ankles, but she was quick and, crouching for a small second on the narrow sill, she dipped her head and sidled through the window into the wash-room.

Nicholas immediately supposed she had done this in an attempt to rescue one of the girls, or assist their escape through the window.

'Come back out here, Selina,' he shouted, heaving himself up to see through the slit. 'It's dangerous. You can't help anybody.'

Selina was pushing her way through the standing group. They moved to give way without resistance. They were silent, except for Tilly, who now sobbed convulsively without tears, her eyes, like the other eyes, wide and fixed on Nicholas with the importance of fear.

Nicholas said, 'The men are coming to open the skylight. They'll be here in a moment. Are there any others of you who would be able to get through the window here? I'll give them a hand. Hurry up, the sooner the better.'

Joanna held a tape-measure in her hand. At some time in the interval between the firemen's discovery that the

99

skylight was firmly sealed and this moment, Joanna had rummaged in one of these top bedrooms to find this tape-measure, with which she had measured the hips of the other ten trapped with herself, even the most helpless, to see what were their possibilities of escape by the seven-inch window slit. It was known all through the club that thirty-six and a quarter inches was the maximum for hips that could squeeze themselves through it, but as the exit had to be effected sideways with a manoeuvring of shoulders, much depended on the size of the bones, and on the texture of the individual flesh and muscles, whether flexible enough to compress easily or whether too firm. The latter had been Tilly's case. But apart from her, none of the women now left on the top floor was slim in anything like the proportions of Selina, Anne, and Pauline Fox. Some were plump. Jane was fat, Dorothy Markham, who had previously been able to slither in and out of the window to sunbathe, was now two months pregnant; her stomach was taut with an immovable extra inch. Joanna's efforts to measure them had been like a scientific ritual in a hopeless case, it had been a something done, it provided a slightly calming distraction.

Nicholas said, 'They won't be long. The men are coming now.' He was hanging on to the ledge of the window with his toes dug into the brickwork of the wall. He was looking towards the edge of the flat roof where the fire ladders were set. A file of firemen were now mounting the ladders with pick-axes, and heavy drills were being hauled up.

Nicholas looked back into the wash-room.

'They're coming now. Where did Selina go?'

No one answered.

He said, 'That girl over there – can't she manage to come through the window?'

He meant Tilly. Jane said, 'She's tried once. She got stuck. The fire's crackling like mad down there. The house is going to collapse any minute.'

In the sloping roof above the girls' heads the picks started to clack furiously at the brick-work, not in regular rhythm as in normal workmanship, but with the desperate hack-work of impending danger. It would not be long, now, before the whistles would blow and the voice from the megaphone would order the firemen to abandon the building to its collapse.

Nicholas had let go his hold to observe the situation from the outside. Tilly appeared at the slit window, now, in a second attempt to get out. He recognised her face as that of the girl who had been stuck there at the moment before the explosion, and whom he had been summoned to release. He shouted at her to get back lest she should stick again, and jeopardise her more probable rescue through the skylight. But she was frantic with determination, she yelled to urge herself on. It was a successful performance after all. Nicholas pulled her clear, breaking one of her hip-bones in the process. She fainted on the flat roof after he had set her down.

He pulled himself up to the window once more. The girls huddled, trembling and silent, round Joanna. They were looking up at the skylight. Some large thing cracked slowly on a lower floor of the house and smoke now started to curl in the upper air of the wash-rooms. Nicholas then saw, through the door of the wash-room, Selina approaching along the smoky passage. She was carrying something fairly long and limp and evidently light in weight, enfolding it carefully in her arms. He thought it was a body. She pushed her way through the girls coughing delicately from the first waves of smoke that had reached her in the passage. The others stared, shivering only with their prolonged apprehension, for they had no curiosity about what she had been rescuing or what she was carrying. She climbed up on the lavatory seat and slid through the window, skilfully and quickly pulling her object behind her. Nicholas held up his hand to catch her. When she landed on the roof-top she said, 'Is it safe out here?' and at the same time was inspecting the condition of her salvaged item. Poise is perfect balance. It was the Schiaparelli dress. The coat-hanger dangled from the dress like a headless neck and shoulders.

'Is it safe out here?' said Selina.

'Nowhere's safe,' said Nicholas.

Later, reflecting on this lightning scene, he could not trust his memory as to whether he then involuntarily signed himself with the cross. It seemed to him, in recollection, that he did. At all events, Felix Dobell, who had appeared on the roof again, looked at him curiously at the time, and later said that Nicholas had crossed himself in superstitious relief that Selina was safe.

She ran to the hotel hatch. Felix Dobell had taken up Tilly in his arms, for although she had recovered consciousness she was too injured to walk. He bore her to the roof-hatch, following Selina with her dress; it was now turned inside-out for safe-keeping.

From the slit window came a new sound, faint, because of the continuous tumble of hose-water, the creak of smouldering wood and plaster in the lower part of the house, and, above, the clamour and falling bricks of the rescue work on the skylight. This new sound rose and fell with a broken hum between the sounds of desperate choking coughs. It was Joanna, mechanically reciting the evening psalter of Day 27, responses and answers.

The voice through the megaphone shouted, 'Tell them to stand clear of the skylight in there. We'll have it free any minute now. It might collapse inwards. Tell those girls to stand clear of the skylight.'

Nicholas climbed up to the window. They had heard the instructions and were already crowding into the lavatory by the slit window, ignoring the man's face that kept appearing in it. As if hypnotised, they surrounded Joanna, and she herself stood as one hypnotised into the strange utterances of Day 27 in the Anglican order, held to be applicable to all sorts and conditions of human life in the world at that particular moment, when in London homing workers plodded across the park, observing with curiosity the fire-engines in the distance, when Rudi Bittesch was sitting in his flat at St John's Wood trying, without success, to telephone to Jane at the club to speak to her privately, the Labour Government was new-born, and elsewhere on the face of the globe people slept, queued for liberation-rations, beat the tom-toms, took shelter from the bombers, or went for a ride on a dodgem at the fun-fair.

Nicholas shouted, 'Keep well away from the skylight. Come right in close to the window.'

The girls crowded into the lavatory space. Jane and Joanna, being the largest, stood up on the lavatory seat to make room for the others. Nicholas saw that every face was streaming with perspiration. Joanna's skin, now close to his eyes, seemed to him to have become suddenly covered with large freckles as if fear had acted on it like the sun; in fact it was true that the pale freckles on her face, which normally were almost invisible, stared out in bright gold spots by contrast with her skin, which was now bloodless with fear. The versicles and responses came from her lips and tongue through the din of demolition.

Yea, the Lord hath done great things for us already: whereof, we rejoice.

Turn our captivity, O Lord: as the rivers in the south.

They that sow in tears: shall reap in joy.

Why, and with what intention, was she moved to indulge in this? She remembered the words, and she had the long habit of recitation. But why, in this predicament and as if to an audience? She wore a dark green wool jersey and a grey skirt. The other girls, automatically listening to Joanna's voice as they had always done, were possibly less frantic and trembled less, because of it, but they turned their ears more fearfully and attentively to the meaning of the skylight noises than they did to the actual meaning of her words for Day 27.

Except the Lord build the house: their labour is but lost that build it.

Except the Lord keep the city: the watchman waketh but in vain.

It is but lost labour that ye haste to rise up early, and so late take rest, and eat the bread of carefulness: for so he giveth his beloved sleep.

Lo, children . . .

Any Day's liturgy would have been equally mesmeric. But the words for the right day was Joanna's habit. The skylight thudded open with a shower of powdery plaster and some lop-sided bricks. While the white dust was still falling the firemen's ladder descended. First up was Dorothy Markham, the chattering débutante whose bright life, for the past forty-three minutes, had gone into a bewildering darkness like illuminations at a seaside town when the electricity system breaks down. She looked haggard and curiously like her aunt, Lady Julia, the chairman of the club's committee who was at that moment innocently tying up refugee parcels at Bath. Lady Julia's hair was white, and so now was the hair of her niece Dorothy, covered as it was by falling plaster-dust, as she clambered up the fire-ladder to the sloping tiles and was assisted to the safe flat roof-top. At her heels came Nancy Riddle, the daughter of the Low-Church Midlands clergyman, whose accents of speech had been in process of improvement by Joanna's lessons. Her elocution days were over now, she would always speak with a Midlands accent. Her hips looked more dangerously wide than they had ever noticeably been, as she swung up the ladder behind Dorothy. Three girls then attempted to follow at once; they had been occupants of a four-bed dormitory on the third floor, and were all newly released from the Forces; all three had the hefty, built-up appearance that five years in the Army was apt to give to a woman. While they were sorting themselves out, Jane grasped the ladder and got away. The three ex-warriors then followed.

Joanna had jumped down from the lavatory seat. She was now circling round, vaguely wobbling, like a top near the end of its spin. Her eyes shifted from the skylight to the window in a puzzled way. Her lips and tongue continued to recite compulsively the litany of the Day, but her voice had weakened and she stopped to cough. The air was still full of powdered plaster and smoke. There were three girls left beside herself. Joanna groped for the ladder and missed. She then stopped to pick up the tape-measure which was lying on the floor. She groped for it as if she were partially blind, still intoning:

So that they who go by say not so much as, The Lord pros-
per you: we wish you good luck in the Name of the Lord.
Out of the deep have I called . . .

The other three took the ladder, one of them, a surprisingly slender girl called Pippa, whose non-apparent bones had evidently been too large to have allowed her escape through the window, shouted back, 'Hurry up, Joanna.'

'Joanna, the ladder!'

And Nicholas shouted from the window, 'Joanna, get up the ladder.'

She regained her senses and pressed behind the last two girls, a brown-skinned heavily-sinewed swimmer and a voluptuous Greek exile of noble birth, both of whom were crying with relief. Joanna promptly started to clamber after them, grasping in her hand a rung that the last girl's foot had just left. At that moment, the house trembled and the ladder and wash-room with it. The fire was extinguished, but the gutted house had been finally thrown by the violence of the work on the skylight. A whistle sounded as Joanna was half-way up. A voice from the megaphone ordered the men to jump clear. The house went down as the last fireman waited at the skylight for Joanna to emerge. As the sloping roof began to cave in, he leapt clear, landing badly and painfully on the flat roof-top. The house sank into its centre, a high heap of rubble, and Joanna went with it.

9

The tape-recording had been erased for economy reasons, so that the tape could be used again. That is how things were in 1945. Nicholas was angry in excess of the occasion. He had wanted to play back Joanna's voice to her father who had come up to London after her funeral to fill in forms as to the effects of the dead. Nicholas had written to him, partly with an urge to impart his last impressions of Joanna, partly from curiosity, partly, too, from a desire to stage a dramatic play-back of Joanna doing *The Wreck of the Deutschland*. He had mentioned the tape-recording in his letter.

But it was gone. It must have been wiped out by someone at his office.

Thou hast bound bones and veins in me, fastened me flesh,
And after it almost unmade, what with dread,
   Thy doing: and dost thou touch me afresh?

Nicholas said to the rector, 'It's infuriating. She was at her best in *The Wreck of the Deutschland*. I'm terribly sorry.'

Joanna's father sat, pink-faced and white-haired. He said, 'Oh, please don't worry.'

'I wish you could have heard it.'

As if to console Nicholas in his loss, the rector murmured with a nostalgic smile:

It was the schooner Hesperus
That sailed the wintry sea,

'No, no, the *Deutschland. The Wreck of the Deutschland.*'

'Oh, the *Deutschland.*' With a gesture characteristic of the English aquiline nose, his seemed to smell the air for enlightenment.

Nicholas was moved by this to a last effort to regain the lost recording. It was a Sunday, but he managed to get one of his colleagues on the telephone at home.

'Do you happen to know if anyone removed a tape from that box I borrowed from the office? Like a fool I left it in my room at the office. Someone's removed an important tape. Something private.'

'No, I don't think . . . just a minute . . . yes, in fact, they've wiped out the stuff. It was poetry. Sorry, but the economy regulations, you know . . . What do you think of the news? Takes your breath away, doesn't it?'

Nicholas said to Joanna's father, 'Yes, it really has been wiped out.'

'Never mind. I remember Joanna as she was in the rectory. Joanna was a great help in the parish. Her coming to London was a mistake, poor girl.'

Nicholas refilled the man's glass with whisky and started to add water. The clergyman signed irritably with his hand to convey the moment when the drink was to his taste. He had the mannerisms of a widower of long years, or of one unaccustomed to being in the company of critical women. Nicholas perceived that the man had never seen the reality of his daughter. Nicholas was consoled for the blighting of his show; the man might not have recognised Joanna in the *Deutschland.*

The frown of his face
Before me, the hurtle of hell
Behind, where, where was a, where was a place?

'I dislike London. I never come up unless I've got to,' the clergyman said, 'for convocation or something like that. If only Joanna could have settled down at the rectory . . . She was restless, poor girl.' He gulped his whisky like a gargle, tossing back his head.

Nicholas said, 'She was reciting some sort of office just before she went down. The other girls were with her, they were listening in a way. Some psalms.'

'Really? No one else has mentioned it.' The old man looked embarrassed. He swirled his drink and swallowed it down, as if Nicholas might be going on to tell him that his daughter had gone over to Rome at the last, or somehow died in bad taste.

Nicholas said violently, 'Joanna had religious strength.'

'I know that, my boy,' said the father, surprisingly.

'She had a sense of Hell. She told a friend of hers that she was afraid of Hell.'

'Really? I didn't know that. I've never heard her speak morbidly. It must have been the influence of London. I never come here, myself, unless I've got to. I had a curacy once, in Balham, in my young days. But since then I've had country parishes. I prefer country parishes. One finds better, more devout, and indeed in some cases, quite holy souls in the country parishes.'

Nicholas was reminded of an American acquaintance of his, a psycho-analyst who had written to say he intended to practise in England after the war, 'away from all these neurotics and this hustling scene of anxiety'.

'Christianity is all in the country parishes these days,' said this shepherd of the best prime mutton. He put down his glass as if to seal his decision on the matter, his grief for the loss of Joanna turning back, at every sequence, on her departure from the rectory.

He said, 'I must go and see the spot where she died.'

Nicholas had already promised to take him to the demolished house in Kensington Road. The father had reminded Nicholas of this several times as if afraid he might inattentively leave London with this duty unfulfilled.

'I'll walk along with you.'

'Well, if it's not out of your way I'll be much obliged. What do you make of this new bomb? Do you think it's only propaganda stuff?'

'I don't know, sir,' said Nicholas.

'It leaves one breathless with horror. They'll have to make an armistice if it's true.' He looked around him as they walked towards Kensington. 'These bomb-sites look tragic. I never come up if I can help it, you know.'

Nicholas said, presently, 'Have you seen any of the girls who were trapped in the house with Joanna, or any of the other members of the club?'

The rector said, 'Yes, quite a few. Lady Julia was kind enough to have a few to tea to meet me yesterday afternoon. Of course, those poor girls have been through an ordeal, even the onlookers among them. Lady Julia suggested we didn't discuss the actual incident. You know, I think that was wise.'

'Yes. Do you recall the girls' names at all?'

'There was Lady Julia's niece, Dorothy, and a Miss Baberton who escaped, I believe, through a window. Several others.'

'A Miss Redwood? Selina Redwood?'

'Well, you know, I'm rather bad at names.'

'A very tall, very slender girl, very beautiful. I want to find her. Dark hair.'

'They were all charming, my dear boy. All young people are charming. Joanna was, to me, the most charming of all, but there I'm partial.'

'She was charming,' said Nicholas, and held his peace.

But the man had sensed his pursuit with the ease of the pastoral expert on home ground, and he inquired solicitously, 'Has this young girl disappeared?'

'Well, I haven't been able to trace her. I've been trying for the past nine days.'

'How odd. She couldn't have lost her memory, I suppose? Wandering the streets . . . ?'

'I think she would have been found in that case. She's very conspicuous.'

'What does her family report?'

'Her family are in Canada.'

'Perhaps she's gone away to forget. It would be understandable. Was she one of the girls who were trapped?'

'Yes. She got out through a window.'

'Well, I don't think she was at Lady Julia's from your description. You could telephone and ask.'

'I have telephoned, in fact. She hasn't heard anything of Selina and neither have any of the other girls. But I was hoping they might be mistaken. You know how it is.'

'Selina . . .' said the rector.

'Yes, that's her name.'

'Just a moment. There was a mention of a Selina. One of the girls, a fair girl, very young, was complaining that Selina had gone off with her only ball dress. Would that be the girl?'

'That's the girl.'

'Not very nice of her to pinch another girl's dress, especially when they've all lost their wardrobes in the fire.'

'It was a Schiaparelli dress.'

The rector did not intrude on this enigma. They came to the site of the May of Teck Club. It looked now like one of the familiar ruins of the neighbourhood, as if it had been shattered years ago by a bomb-attack, or months ago by a guided missile. The paving stones of the porch lay crookedly leading nowhere. The pillars lay like Roman remains. A side wall at the back of the house stood raggedly at half its former height. Greggie's garden was a heap of masonry with a few flowers and rare plants sprouting from it. The pink and white tiles of the hall lay in various aspects of long neglect, and from a lower part of the ragged side wall a piece of brown drawing-room wall-paper furled more raggedly.

Joanna's father stood holding his wide black hat.

At the top of the house the apples are laid in rows,

The rector said to Nicholas. 'There's really nothing to see.'

'Like my tape-recording,' said Nicholas.

'Yes, it's all gone, all elsewhere.'

Rudi Bittesch lifted and flicked through a pile of notebooks that lay on Nicholas's table. He said, 'Is this the manuscript of your book by the way?'

He would not have taken this liberty in the normal course, but Nicholas was under a present obligation to him. Rudi had discovered the whereabouts of Selina.

'You can have it,' said Nicholas, meaning the manuscript.

He said, not foreseeing the death he was to die, 'You can keep it. It might be valuable one day when I'm famous.'

Rudi smiled. All the same, he tucked the books under his arm and said, 'Coming along?'

On the way to pick up Jane to go and see the fun at the Palace, Nicholas said, 'Anyway, I've decided not to publish the book. The typescripts are destroyed.'

'I have this bloody big lot of books to carry, and now you tell me this. What value to me if you don't publish?'

'Keep them, you never know.'

Rudi had a caution about these things. He kept *The Sabbath Notebooks*, eventually to reap his reward.

'Would you like a letter from Charles Morgan to me saying I'm a genius?' Nicholas said.

'You're bloody cheerful about something or other.'

'I know,' said Nicholas. 'Would you like to have the letter, though?'

'What letter?'

'Here it is.' Nicholas brought Jane's letter from his inside pocket, crumpled like a treasured photograph.

Rudi glanced at it. 'Jane's work,' he said, and handed it back. 'Why are you so cheerful? Did you see Selina?'

'Yes.'

'What did she say?'

'She screamed. She couldn't stop screaming. It's a nervous reaction.'

'The sight of you must have brought all back to her. I advised you to keep away.'

'She couldn't stop screaming.'

'You frightened her.'

'Yes.'

'I said keep away. She's no good, by the way, with a crooner in Clarges Street. You see him?'

'Yes, he's a perfectly nice chap. They're married.'

'So they say. You want to find a girl with character. Forget her.'

'Oh, well. Anyway, he was very apologetic about her screaming, and I was very apologetic, of course. It made her scream more. I think she'd have preferred to see a fight.'

'You don't love her that much, to fight a crooner.'

'He was quite a decent crooner.'

'You heard him croon?'

'No, of course, that's a point.'

Jane was restored to her normal state of unhappiness and hope, and was now established in a furnished room in Kensington Church Street. She was ready to join them.

Rudi said, 'You don't scream when you see Nicholas?'

'No,' she said, 'but if he goes on refusing to let George publish his book I will scream. George is putting the blame on me. I told him about the letter from Charles Morgan.'

'You should fear him,' Rudi said. 'He makes ladies scream by the way. Selina got a fright from him today.'

'I got a fright from her last time.'

'Have you found her then?' said Jane.

'Yes, but she's suffering from shock. I must have brought all the horrors back to her mind.'

'It was hell,' Jane said.

'I know.'

'Why is he in love with Selina by the way?' Rudi said. 'Why doesn't he find a woman of character or a French girl?'

'This is a toll call,' Jane said, rapidly.

'I know. Who's speaking?' said Nancy, the daughter of the Midlands clergyman, now married to another Midlands clergyman.

'It's Jane. Look, I've just got another question to ask you, quickly, about Nicholas Farringdon. Do you think his conversion had anything to do with the fire? I've got to finish this big article about him.'

'Well, I always like to think it was Joanna's example. Joanna was very High Church.'

'But he wasn't in love with Joanna, he was in love with Selina. After the fire he looked for her all over the place.'

'Well, he couldn't have been converted by Selina. Not converted.'

'He's got a note in his manuscript that a vision of evil may be as effective to conversion as a vision of good.'

'I don't understand these fanatics. There's the pips, Jane. I think he was in love with us all, poor fellow.'

The public swelled on V.J. night of August as riotously as on the victory night of May. The little figures appeared duly on the balcony every half-hour, waved for a space and disappeared.

Jane, Nicholas and Rudi were suddenly in difficulties, being pressed by the crowd from all sides. 'Keep your elbows out if possible,' Jane and Nicholas said to each other, almost simultaneously; but this was useless advice. A seaman, pressing on Jane, kissed her passionately on the mouth; nothing whatsoever could be done about it. She was at the mercy of his wet beery mouth until the crowd gave way, and then the three pressed a path to a slightly healthier spot, with access to the park.

Here, another seaman, observed only by Nicholas, slid a knife silently between the ribs of a woman who was with him. The lights went up on the balcony, and a hush anticipated the Royal appearance. The stabbed woman did not scream, but sagged immediately. Someone else screamed through the hush, a woman, many yards away, some other victim. Or perhaps that screamer had only had her toes trodden upon. The crowd began to roar again. All their eyes were at this moment fixed on the Palace balcony, where the Royal family had appeared in due order. Rudi and Jane were busy yelling their cheers.

Nicholas tried unsuccessfully to move his arm above the crowd to draw attention to the wounded woman. He had been shouting that a woman had been stabbed. The seaman was shouting accusations at his limp woman, who was still kept upright by the crowd. These private demonstrations faded in the general pandemonium. Nicholas was borne away in a surge that pressed from the Mall. When the balcony darkened, he was again able to make a small clearing through the crowd, followed by Jane and Rudi towards the open park. On the way, Nicholas was forced to a standstill and found himself close by the knifer. There was no sign of the wounded woman. Nicholas, waiting to move, took the letter from Charles Morgan from his pocket and thrust it down the seaman's blouse, and then was borne onwards. He did this for no apparent reason and to no effect, except that it was a gesture. That is the way things were at that time.

They walked back through the clear air of the park, step-ping round the couples who lay locked together in their path. The park was filled with singing. Nicholas and his companions sang too. They ran into a fight between British and American servicemen. Two men lay unconscious at the side of the path, being tended by their friends. The crowds cheered in the distance behind them. A formation of aircraft buzzed across the night sky. It was a glorious victory.

Jane mumbled, 'Well, I wouldn't have missed it, really.' She had halted to pin up her straggling hair, and had a hair-pin in her mouth as she said it. Nicholas marvelled at her stamina, recalling her in this image years later in the country of his death – how she stood, sturdy and bare-legged on the dark grass, occupied with her hair – as if this was an image of all the May of Teck establishment in its meek, unselfconscious attitudes of poverty, long ago in 1945.